A Bang

Land of Poisoned Smiles Trilogy

Book 1

Written and published by Alexander Menyharth

Amazon Edition

Cover image by Simon Bird

Copyright 2023 Alexander Menyharth

Dedication

To all the enchanting Thai girls who have so enlightened and enriched my travel experiences.

To Heidi,
Hope you enjoy!
— Alex M.
x

1 – Arrival

He had made it. He had finally *made* it.

Damian Shaw stumbled out of the trademark yellow and green Bangkok taxi cab, muttering an ill-pronounced Thai 'thank you' to the driver. From the garish neon lights, blaring western pop music and the shrill shouts of the girls, there was no mistaking that this was the legendary Soi Cowboy, as described by his more than enthusiastic student friends.

"You'll bloody love it, mate!" Jason had drawled in the student union bar over his sixth pint of Holsten Pils, mopping the unkempt red hair from his glazed eyes. "The girls there can't get enough of it!"

"You're English, man. They love the English!" Josh had added, after a moment's thought.

"You'll finally get laid!" Kevin had jibed through a mouthful of pork scratchings.

These comments had irked Damian at first, but the more his friends had boasted about their own experiences, the more his fantasies were fuelled with this exotic culture full of beautiful golden-skinned girls who just wanted to make love to western men. After his graduation, he had discussed his future with his Aunt Claire. In the absence of his parents – who spent most of their time overseas on business – Claire had taken care of Damian and his sister, and, most certainly, become like a second mother to them. She had given Damian a generous financial gift to secure a career, and to – as she had succinctly put it – 'see a bit of this weird and wonderful world!' And so, waking up one night in his cramped, dark London bedsit – restless with loneliness, loins burning – he had looked out of his rain smeared window and decided to – finally – take the plunge.

After a thirteen-hour flight, sandwiched between an overweight and over-talkative Geordie and a mother more concerned with her laptop than her screaming kid, he had landed at Bangkok's Suvarnabhumi Airport from which he had just about managed to navigate the taxi driver – who, of course, spoke no English – through the congested city traffic to his hotel. That evening, trying to ignore the creeping sensations of jet lag, he had found the way to his ultimate destination.

Damian took a deep breath, and, coughing slightly from exhaust fumes, strolled bravely into the melee. Immediately, the petite girls were laughing and tugging at his arm in an attempt to entice him into their respective clubs or bars, and Damian self-consciously noticed a group of khaki-clad police loitering on the corner smoking cigarettes. However, as fortune would have it, he soon found himself within the confines of the much talked about Country Road bar. It was, indeed, just as his friends had described it: a dark enclave of thumping loud rock music, packed full of beautiful Thai girls with western men shouting, dancing and playing pool.

Damian was ushered to the bar, where he plonked down on a stool right next to the all-girl live band. The noise was quite deafening from this proximity, but Damian could not care. He felt a thrill of exhilaration from the electric atmosphere, and quickly downed a cool bottle of Heineken served to him by one of the smiling waitresses dressed in American cowboy-like attire. The beat of the music pulsed through him, and it was not long before he felt a connection with the swaying, gyrating bodies all about him.

Although, as he watched, he could not help but notice how old many of the men were and how seemingly intoxicated the young girls were dancing with them. His eyes were soon drawn to a particularly sexy looking girl who was dancing with happy wild abandon on her own. She was wearing a tight, black all-in-one skirt, and, as she ground her body, arms above her head, Damian felt a flush of excitement as he noticed her well-formed treacle-coloured breasts spilling forth from it whenever she bent forward. Now she was facing the band, her arms still raised, and his eyes moved to her pert bottom, jiggling as she jumped up and down. Damian ordered himself another beer and almost choked on it as he turned back just in time to see the girl reveal a distinct lack of panties as she stooped over to try and clamber up onto the music stage. Another girl quickly pulled her skirt back down in an attempt to preserve her modesty, and one of the musicians good-humouredly pushed her back onto the dance floor. Damian's eyes boggled as the girl abruptly turned and kissed the girl who had helped her on the mouth. The men whooped in delight, and the two girls, enjoying the appreciation, began a close dance together. Damian just wished Jason and the guys could be here to see this. He continued to watch mesmerized as the two girls rubbed their bodies up against one another. It was then that he caught the eye of the girl who had been exhibiting herself and he quickly looked away embarrassed.

Damian finished his beer and felt a need for the toilet. He saw the necessary sign emblazoned by a red neon light at the other side of the bar past the dance floor and the pool tables. The two girls were now lost in the crowd of dancers and Damian carefully pushed his way through the sweating throng. The male toilet was indicated by a picture on the door of a stick man complete with a stick male appendage. A stick woman with long hair and circles and dots denoting breasts marked the adjacent female toilet door. On entering the toilet, Damian was surprised to be greeted by a swarthy man holding white towels over his arm. Feeling a bit awkward, he positioned himself at the urinal with his back facing the man. To make matters more difficult, he found he was still a bit swollen down there after watching that girl and he had trouble manoeuvring himself out from his fly.

"Hi, handsome. Do you need some help?" a sultry voice said from behind.

Damian froze for a moment, and then glanced over his shoulder. *It was her!* What was more, the man had gone. They were alone. He felt his heart quickening. *What the hell was he going to do?! What would Jason do?!*

"Yes. I need some help!" he heard himself splutter.

A Bangkok Fairy Tale

The girl needed no further encouragement and obligingly slipped her hand into his fly and gently held him over the urinal with soft, cool fingers. Damian could not believe this was happening to him. Unfortunately, the excitement had now become too much and he was unable to relieve himself. He nervously looked towards the door. *Someone was bound to come in – and where was that man with the towels?!*

The girl was giggling. This bizarre situation was obviously not bothering her.

Before Damian could say anything, the girl started to massage his exposed manhood, and then her silken fingers glided smoothly up into his boxers. He swallowed and placed the palms of his hands against the damp wall. *What the hell was going on?!* Part of him wanted her to stop, part wanted her to continue.

Damian glanced back at that wobbling deep cleavage, as her fingers expertly squeezed and stroked him. He had now totally forgotten about his precarious situation as he felt the electric thrill of a climax approaching ...

The door swung open!

"What the fuck's going on in here?" demanded a deep Australian voice.

The shock of absolute humiliation and sexual climax mingled into a blur as Damian grabbed his shorts and boxers that had now fallen to his knees and barged past the girl and the Australian man through the toilet door and into the bar's crowded pool area. He was aware of a chorus of shouts and screams of laughter as he tripped over a pool cue, his face slamming down hard onto the stone tiled floor. The last thing Damian remembered seeing amongst all the surrounding raucous chaos was the girl's laughing face looking down at him …

2 – Awakening

A sea of gleaming Bangkok skyscrapers washed towards him in a gentle tide, the blinking red lights adorning their silver crowns entrancing him. Wisps of streaming cloud began to envelop him in a silky whiteness, beyond which the effervescent form of a girl could be seen dancing, arms raised. He felt himself drifting towards her. Closer ... closer ...

The white cloud gradually formed into curtains, the red lights now belonging to machinery, and the girl ...

"How are you feeling?" the young nurse asked.

Damian Shaw cried out with a start. The nurse was looking down at him, her almond eyes worried. "Wh–what happened ...?" he said, fighting a wave of panic.

"You hurt your head. Now you are in hospital," the nurse replied, accenting the last word of each sentence. "But you OK. You not worry." She touched him reassuringly on the arm, and gave him that endearing Thai smile.

Damian took a deep breath and propped himself up on an elbow. Although his head certainly hurt and he felt dizzy, he began to appreciate the attractive Thai nurse who was so willing to take care of him. She was dressed in white and typically petite and slender, with her dark hair tied back beneath the white cap.

"Now you rest," she said, an aroma of jasmine about her as she stooped over to adjust the bandage, her breast pleasantly brushing against his cheek.

Damian lay back and shut his eyes, trying to remember the previous events. Slowly, but surely, it all came back ... *Soi Cowboy ... the bar toilet ... the girl laughing at him ...*

"Oh ... shit!" he murmured, and fell into a dreamless sleep.

3 – Awareness

The next morning, the stifling blanket of heat hit Damian as he left the cool haven of air conditioning that was Bangkok Hospital. Ahead of him a marketplace shimmered in the haze, like an approaching mirage. Thai people were now bustling about him – he seemed to be the only westerner – and his aching head was overwhelmed with the sound of motorcycles buzzing like some huge monstrous insects and the plaintive cries of the women selling their wares. The humid air seemed to heighten the smells of the strong spices, cooking meat, sweat and sewers, adding to a mounting feeling of suffocation. The colours of the unrecognizable fruit and vegetables adorning the stalls were striking, and, as he fanned himself with his T-shirt, he realized how hungry he had become and grabbed a chocolate and banana pancake from one of the street vendors before dipping into an internet café behind the market. He pushed past some fat kids lost in their own worlds of computer gaming and managed to find an empty seat, fortunately near a fan. Damian had left his phone behind in the hotel, but, as he had hoped, the computers here had Skype facilities, and Jason was online.

"What the hell happened to you? You look like shit!" Jason said, munching noisily on a packet of crisps.

Despite the coarse directness of the greeting, Damian was happy to see a familiar face. He scratched at his itching scalp beneath the bandage. "You're not gonna believe this!"

Damian related the whole story, as far as he could remember, to his friend.

Jason gave one of his annoyingly condescending laughs. "You've gotta be kidding me!"

"It's true! I'm telling you!"

"Then you've been stitched up, mate!"

Damian's heart sank. It had occurred to him that it could have been a setup, but he was foolishly hoping his friend would reassure him otherwise. "Come on. How can you know that for sure?"

"It happens all the time over there! Have you got your money and passport?"

"Yeah. Nothing's been taken!"

"Then you're a lucky bastard! Take my advice – go back to the hospital and shag the nurse!"

"Piss off!"

Jason's mocking expression was now serious. "I know you, Damie. You're gonna go back and look for this bitch, aren't you?"

Damian had considered this. "Maybe."

Jason impatiently shoved aside his crisps packet. "Don't! I mean it! You won't be so bloody lucky next time!"

Damian, all of a sudden, felt very tired. "Look," he sighed. "I'll be really careful. Promise."

Jason snorted derisively. "Oh yeah? Like hell!"

"I'll keep you posted."

Jason shook his head in resignation. "Just make sure you *are* damn well careful!"

4 – Attitude

The Udomsuk Hotel was a faceless concrete structure as remote and cold in its appearance as those lost souls that sought its shelter. It was recognized locally as a seedy establishment of ill-repute, acting as a refuge for desperate men and eager prostitutes; a sleazy den of clandestine seduction for disloyal husbands and their mistresses; a place of anonymity, where sexual fantasies could be played out and forgotten. To the likes of Damian Shaw, filled with the naive ignorance of an incongruent culture, it was simply adequate for his short-term needs. It was cheap and situated in a relatively quiet area, set back from the main road and on the outskirts of the city, not too far from the airport.

The room he had was certainly basic with little more than a bed, table, chair, small wardrobe and adjoining bathroom.

A Bangkok Fairy Tale

The air conditioning did not seem to be working. He did not even have a door key, having to inform one of the blue-aproned female members of staff whenever he wanted to return to his room. There was, fortunately, a telephone for room service on the table, and a satellite TV was fixed below the low ceiling. After sleeping for most of the day, he had visited an internet café across the road where he had managed to grab a cup of coffee and send the obligatory emails to his parents, aunt and sister, discreetly omitting any mention of girls or accidents for the time being. He now threw off his sweat soaked T-shirt and switched the TV on, managing to find a fuzzy American channel. He went into the bathroom and looked in the cracked mirror, wincing at his unshaven features and bleary eyes. The bandage looked dirty and had slipped over his left eye. He carefully unpinned and removed it, and then looked back in the mirror to assess the damage. There was a large bump caked in dry blood and it was sore to the touch. Grimacing, he tousled his tawny hair and splashed water over his face. There was a separate tiled cubicle for the shower and he stepped into it, letting the cold water clean the wound and refresh him – washing away the humiliation and shame of the previous evening and allowing him the clarity of planning a next move. He downed a couple of the Paracetamol tablets the nurse had given him with a bottle of water from his rucksack, and laid out some fresh clothes on the bed.

The blurred events of Soi Cowboy began to spin through his mind again, and he tried to make some sense of them. *Who was that girl? He needed to know!* He felt himself becoming aroused once more, as he remembered the caress of those cool, gentle fingers. *He had to find her!* But, was Jason right, and it was all a setup? The cold, stinging memory returned of all those bastards laughing at him. *Was that Australian guy her boyfriend? What happened to the man with the towels? How did he get to the hospital?* What was more – *did he have the nerve to show his face in that bar again?* He felt a burning tinge of anger. *Too damn right he did!*

He cleaned his teeth, gargled some Listerine, and got dressed in a clean white T-shirt, khaki shorts, leather sandals, and imitation Rolex he had picked up for a snip at a market stall earlier. He looked in the mirror again. *OK. Looking better, my friend!* He walked over to the stained, grimy window in the bedroom and it gave a protesting creak as he opened it. The evening sky was darkening, an amber moon hanging above the twinkling silver skyscrapers. In the foreground were shops and apartments about which the Thai people were scurrying about their business in the receding light. He took in a deep breath of the humid air, cleaner than the city centre. *Right Bangkok! This time I'm ready for you!*

He shut the window, and then noticed he had lost the channel coverage on the TV. Irritated, he grabbed the remote to see if he could find another channel. He managed to get a clear picture. It showed two naked Asian girls enjoying themselves with what looked like a selection of sex toys. *Jesus! He had found a porn channel!* Curiosity getting the better of him, he continued to watch. His heart quickened as he imagined himself watching the girl from Soi Cowboy. *No! She wasn't like that!* He felt suddenly protective towards her. Annoyed with himself, he switched the TV off. *He had to see her again ...!*

5 – Return

The taxi ride seemed to take forever, partly due to the weekend early evening traffic congestion, but mostly due to the mounting tension and discomfort Damian was feeling about his return to Soi Cowboy. The driver had been helpful, adjusting his seat and turning on the radio, but Damian hardly noticed. He was once again rehearsing the conversation he would have with the girl: *'Why did you do that?'... 'I thought you liked me!'... 'Why did you laugh at me?'... 'Was your boyfriend there?'... 'Who are you?'* The chances were she would not be around tonight anyway. This thought calmed him slightly. In which case, he would just apologize to the bar staff at Country Road and find out what had happened from them. Then he would be free to enjoy his holiday again, and find some other girls. Damian smiled to himself. Yes. Everything will work out fine after all …

"Soi Cowboy," the taxi driver informed him.

Damian took a deep breath. "OK. Thanks."

He fumbled through his wallet and pulled out two hundred-baht notes to pay the driver before climbing out of the car. He looked around to orientate himself. The neon lights, crowds of westerners and excitable Thai girls were there, but he did not recognize the bars. To his left, where Country Road should be, were a couple of European themed pubs: one English, one Dutch. Then he remembered from the internet map he had downloaded during his pre-flight research that he was on Sukhumvit Soi 23 perpendicular to the other end of Soi Cowboy. Oh well. At least this gave him the chance to explore the whole of the Soi, which he had been unable to do before.

Out of curiosity, Damian was drawn towards the English pub that was slightly further along the Sukhumvit road. The building was certainly anglicized enough to look like a convincing town or village pub from anywhere in the British Isles, complete with a white wall latticed with black beams and a large curved bay window. Next to the entrance was an old-fashioned door lamp and above were big gold letters proclaiming the name 'The Ship Inn'. The door was open and he found the interior to be equally as authentic. It was quite a darkened environment with benches, tables and chairs positioned as they would in any normal pub, and there was a large wooden framed picture of a sailing ship hanging from the wall and a model of a similar vessel in a glass case on a shelf above the bay window. There were wooden stools about the bar, upon which sat a western couple, but, of course, where the facade fell apart was the obvious absence of any British real ale – only European and Thai lager, and the ubiquitous Irish Guinness – and the bar staff were mostly smartly dressed Thai girls.

Damian went to the bar, and, for a change, ordered himself a small Guinness. After all, it seemed like the closest beer to a British beer. He sat at a table by the wall above which was an antiquated looking golfing advert celebrating Johnnie Walker – *'the whisky that goes with a swing!'* The place was relatively quiet compared to the crowds milling about Soi Cowboy, and Damian found himself again craving for the excitement of Bangkok proper. He would find no clue to his sexy quarry here. He quickly downed the lacklustre stout – he had tasted the real stuff in Dublin – and was about to make an exit when he noticed something out of the corner of his eye. Someone was looking directly at him.

He turned to see a dark figure running into the shadows at the back of the pub. Without thinking Damian got to his feet and followed. Maybe he was wrong about finding no clues. He found himself near the bathrooms, and a cold feeling of shame returned as he remembered his last encounter with a Thai public toilet. He could see no one. Whoever it was must have gone into either the male or female room. This time the doors were labelled in English simply as 'Gentlemen' and 'Ladies'. He opened the 'Gentlemen' door. A light automatically came on, but the room was empty. He did the same with the 'Ladies'. Nothing. He looked around again. Maybe he had imagined it. His mind was jittery. He had overreacted. Then he heard a clattering of metallic objects … and froze …

Another door was closing. He saw from the dimly illuminated red sign above that it was the fire escape door and ran over to it, painfully encountering a broom and metal bucket on the way. He pushed the door open and found himself in a car park. In the moonlight he saw the figure running towards the main road. It was small and had long dark hair. *It could be the girl!* Damian was now running fast himself across the car park back to Sukhumvit Soi 23. *Damn!* The girl had gone. Lost to the heaving crowds …

6 – Pursuit

Damian's mind was racing as he allowed the crowds to carry him back in the direction of Soi Cowboy. *That must have been her! Why was she spying on him? How did she know he would be in that pub?*

Someone grabbed his wrist. He jolted as he turned and saw a girl. But it was not her. It was another small, scantily dressed girl from one of the bars. "Come on! Come and see!" she sang.

"Sure. Why not?" Damian said resignedly, and allowed himself to be led through the shouting throng of westerners.

He saw that he was at the beginning of the Soi and he was being taken into one of the large bars on the right. It was the Baccara. Jason and the guys had told him – very excitedly, if he recalled correctly – about this place too. Within the crowded, darkened interior was a large well-lit dance floor with the bikini-clad girls pole dancing. He wandered in with the girl leading him by the hand, and, as with Country Road, let the electric atmosphere and thumping music wash over him. The girl smiled at him and returned to her post at the door. It seemed too crowded to get a seat, and so Damian made his way towards the bar. He looked up at one of the dancing girls as she sensuously raised her arms upwards to the rhythm of the beat, revealing an athletic torso. She brought her arms together, squeezing her ample breasts, beads of sweat just visible. She wore a naked expression of prurience upon a young face that would otherwise look so innocent, with mouth open, yearning and eyes half closed. Damian then remembered what the guys had told him about this place and suddenly looked up further towards the ceiling. *Yes. There they were!*

The bar's floor was two-tiered with the above floor being clear glass and providing, as Josh had so enthusiastically put it, *'the best view in Bangkok!'* And Damian could see why! On the glass floor were more dancers, but dressed as untidy schoolgirls, neck ties loose, shirts half-unbuttoned, hair tied up in bundles. But, what was most exciting on the eye – as became plainly clear to Damian from his vantage point as the girls playfully danced and jumped about – was that beneath the plaid skirts they were obviously wearing no panties! Damian noticed a group of bespectacled Japanese men standing next to him ogling upwards for a flash of the shaven buds of genitalia on display. He grinned to himself as he picked up his beer. *Cheers Josh!*

Feeling somewhat mellower, Damian continued his way through the Soi, only to be grabbed again by another girl. This one, however, was rougher on the arm and yanked Damian to a bar illuminated with the neon yellow name of 'Cockatoo'.

A Bangkok Fairy Tale

Through the curtained entrance he was confronted with a smaller, narrower and dimly lit dance floor on which the six or so dancers were perceptibly far less enthusiastic than the Baccara girls and limply hung from the poles, moving listlessly to the soft background house music with bored expressions on their over made-up faces.

"Please, sit," the girl said, ushering him to a table opposite the dance floor.

Damian obediently did so, and was immediately joined by three other girls. The two girls either side of him rubbed their brown, bikini-clad bodies against him and he looked down at the inviting breasts. *Were they real, or plastic?* A waitress came over, and Damian found himself buying all three girls a drink.

"What is your name?" the girl on his left enquired.

"Damian," he replied.

"Where you come from?" the girl on the right asked.

"England."

"Ohh."

Damian smiled to himself. Well, he had not come here for the scintillating conversation. He raised his glass to the girls, who reciprocated. Damian settled back. He might as well enjoy their company. It cost enough. He raised his eyebrows as the girl on the right grabbed him between the legs. *Oh, what the hell!* He put his hand on the thigh of the girl on his left. She gave him a leering smile, protruding her tongue and licking her upper lip, before guiding his hand upward to her bikini panties. He smiled back, and tentatively inserted his fingers within … and found himself caressing … *something hard?!*

"What the …?!" Damian cried, quickly getting to his feet. He suddenly felt like retching.

Damian staggered out of the bar, not looking back until he was safely outside. Then he noticed that above the bright yellow 'COCKATOO' was the wording in red: 'BANGKOK LADYBOYS'!

"Shit ... fuck ... shit!" he gasped, stooping forward, trying not to gag and not caring about the looks he was getting from the other punters.

He heard a familiar laugh behind him. He whirled round ... and froze. *It was her!*

7 – Encounter

"So. You like boys!" the girl said.

She was standing about ten feet away from Damian, darkly silhouetted against the neon glare of the bars with hands on hips.

Damian looked at her aghast. She had caught him in *another* humiliating predicament. "What? No … I didn't know …"

The girl laughed again. "I think you know."

"No. I was looking for you!" Damian blurted, defensively.

A group of western men in football shirts drunkenly bumped into Damian, almost knocking him over.

"Come," the girl said, gesturing him to follow her.

She ran across the road to the Shark, another large bar adjacent to the Baccara. Damian did not want to lose her again and pushed past some Thai girls, who scowled at him, to keep up.

The Shark had an exterior bar opened out to the Soi from outside the curtained entranceway leading into the dance area. The girl was sitting in the corner, beneath the widescreen TV showing English football, legs crossed and looking over at Damian with a sly, amused expression. She was wearing the same tight black top as the previous night, her generous bosom tantalizingly curving over the brim. Damian was determined to maintain whatever dignity he had left, and tried to stroll as nonchalantly as he could past the large, bear-like western men. He pulled up a stool next to her, his mind suddenly going blank of all the questions he wanted to ask.

"Well. You found me," the girl said, simply.

"I saw you at that pub."

The girl chuckled and looked away.

"What?"

"That was not me. That was my little sister. She see you and come and tell me."

Damian inwardly cursed himself for his foolishness. "Oh. Well … I thought she was too small for you," he replied, clumsily.

The girl chuckled again, covering her mouth with her hand in a way that Damian found quite endearing. "You funny," she said.

Damian took the plunge. "Last night. What happened? Why did you laugh at me?"

At that point, Chelsea conceded a goal, and the girl's response was drowned out by a sea of groans.

Damian was becoming irritated by the harsh surroundings. He bent towards her. "Sorry … What did you say?"

But, the girl was up again, and moving to the entrance of the main bar. "Come and look inside," she said.

"Dammit!" Damian spluttered impatiently. *Where the hell was she off to now?!* And, again, he found himself hurriedly chasing after her.

8 - Illumination

A wave of anxiety came over Damian as he realized the girl had been swallowed up by the swelling crowd. He desperately scanned around the bar, squinting against the flashing lights. The anxiety was replaced by relief as he caught a glimpse of her edging towards the dancing stage. He moved in her direction, beginning to feel more relaxed now that he had her fixed in his sights. The interior of the Shark was similar to that of the Baccara, only slightly smaller. The longitudinal dancing stage was elevated, with the central section revolving like a carousel. There seemed to be too many girls on the stage, and they were jostling against one another, not that they seemed to mind. Damian noticed appreciatively that, this time, the bikinis the girls were wearing were very much see-through. The problem was, however, that with the loud techno music blaring out, along with the bustling horde of revellers, it was going to be even more difficult for him to talk to the girl than on the outside. *He still did not even know her name!*

The girl glanced back at Damian and pointed to a winding metal staircase past the dancing stage. She ran up it and he followed her to a second floor, and to his relief found it much quieter. Here, there were only a couple of unused pool tables with sofas on which a small group of more Japanese men were having some intimate time with a couple of the dancers. The girl beckoned Damian over to a secluded sofa in the corner. He sat down, grateful to be finally alone with her. Now, he could get some answers.

"This is where I work!" the girl said, raising her arms in a graceful demeanour, as if to encompass the whole bar – pool tables, horny Japanese men, and all.

Damian realized that this was the first time he had got a proper look at her – at least, above the neckline. She was certainly pretty and he guessed she must be in her early to mid-twenties, and yet, beneath the mask of make-up and extended eyelashes, he could see signs of an impish little girl, dark eyes darting about, inquisitively taking everything in, with the occasional wiggle of a cute button nose. "So … what happened last night?" he said, trying to sound matter-of-fact as he, again, tried to ask the all-important question.

"We have plenty time to talk, but now – look!" the girl replied, pointing back towards the staircase.

A large girl in one of the see-through bikinis was coming up the steps with a tray of drinks. Damian was side-tracked as this new girl fully caught his attention. Her laughing face was wide-boned, dark hair curling down to heavy breasts all too visible beneath the skimpy material.

"I think you like," the girl said in his ear.

"She's ... very nice," Damian had to admit.

The two girls began to talk excitedly to one another in Thai and the tray was placed on the table in front of Damian. It carried three drinks – two cola-based cocktails, with ice and straws, and a beer he was unfamiliar with. It had a green label on which were depicted two white elephants facing a golden fountain.

"Beer Chang," the smaller girl informed him. "It Thai beer. I think you like."

"OK. Thanks," Damian acknowledged. It was about time he tried a local brew.

The girl serving snuggled next to Damian on his other side, and, again, he found himself totally distracted from what he was trying to say, leaving him still none the wiser about last night's events. *But damn! He had a Thai angel on either side of him!* He nervously took a gulp of the cool beer. It tasted light and refreshing, sweeter than the lager beer he was used to. But the taste was good. *Very good!* He took another swig. A pleasant warmth was coming over him. He was becoming more aware of the throbbing music in the bar below and the overall electric atmosphere of this exciting place ... not to mention the amazingly sexy company he was in! It occurred to him that he might just be getting a little drunk. And yet, he was not feeling any of the incumbent negative effects of being intoxicated, but more a lucid high ... *and he was also beginning to get really horny!* He remembered Jason's warning and cleared his throat in an attempt to keep himself focused.

"I tell her all about you!" confessed the smaller girl, and gently ran her slender fingers over his crutch. "She want to see!"

"See what? Oh!" Damian suddenly realized what she was talking about. He felt flattered, but also a touch embarrassed at being spoken about in such a way. "Thanks, but there's really nothing special about … *mmmph!"*

The big girl had bent over and was kissing him full on the mouth, her tongue pushing towards his throat. Damian was not expecting this. *What the hell should he do now?!* He lay back on the sofa, grabbing a handful of ample bosom to steady himself. Quite easy … *just lie back and enjoy!* But, a paranoid thought jumped into his mind, and he drew his hand down her side and slipped it into her panties. *No! Definitely not a man!*

The girl's hand was fumbling for his fly. Now Damian felt a hint of panic. *Things were going too fast … and he was losing self-control!* He grabbed her wrist. "W–wait a minute!" he managed to mumble, pushing his face away from hers. "Let's just slow down a bit here!"

The big girl laughed. She lay back on the sofa, propping herself up with an elbow.

"She just want to play with you," the smaller girl said. "You not like?"

"Yes, I like," said Damian. "But, you're going too fast. I don't know anything about either of you. Now is the time for us to talk!"

"He not want talk!" she replied, pointing meaningfully at the bulge in his shorts.

"*He* can wait!" retorted Damian.

"OK. You want talk. We talk." The girl sat back, taking a sip from her drink, her eyes glancing up at him solemnly, like some reprimanded schoolgirl.

Damian looked around. The Japanese men were leaving, arms round their female entourage. "Right. Well … what's your name, for a start?"

"My name Nok. It mean bird." She put her hands together to emulate wings, then gestured towards the other girl. "This Mai." The impish glint returned to her eye and she added, laughingly: "She very dirty!"

The big girl's large, lippy mouth grinned back lasciviously.

"What your name?" Nok asked.

"It's Damian. Damian Shaw."

"Please to meet you, Damian … Shoo."

Damian smirked at her mispronunciation, and then took her hand as she held it out to him. He took a long draught of the extraordinary beer. *Great! At last he was getting somewhere!* He was ready to persevere with his questioning. "So … last night … when I first met you. What … happened?"

Nok widened her eyes in surprise. "You not know?"

Damian shrugged, as he tried again to recount the events of that fateful evening. "I … was with you in … the toilet …" He looked away, embarrassed at the memory. "Then … the Australian guy … your boyfriend … or whoever he was …"

"He not my boyfriend."

"Oh." Damian felt a wave of relief. *Maybe he hadn't been set up, after all!* "Right. Well. I panicked … basically."

Nok frowned.

Damian hesitated. *She wasn't understanding him.* "Panicked?" he repeated, and made a worried face, wringing his hands.

The girls laughed. "I see," Nok said.

"I remember falling over … and waking up in hospital." He pointed to the mark at the top of his forehead.

"Yes. You hurt. We call ... am ..." The girl frowned again as she tried to think of the name.

"Ambulance. Yes!" Damian felt a thrill as the mystery unfolded. He was beginning to feel less paranoid. There was, however, still one question he had to ask. "But, why did you laugh at me?"

Nok looked at him quizzically. "I not laugh at you."

"Yes, you did. At the bar ... Country Road."

"Oh. I thinking you drink too much." She put two fingers to her mouth, showing embarrassment. "We take care of you."

Damian thought about this. It all sort of made sense. He must have just freaked out when that Australian guy had wandered into the toilet. And, that towel guy must have just simply left to give them some privacy. *But he had still been caught in the middle of the bar with everyone looking at his ...! What the hell! It was Bangkok!*

"What you think about?" Nok asked.

"I think ... you should show me a bit more of Soi Cowboy!" Damian declared, finishing off his beer.

Nok smiled. "What about ...?" She gestured towards the big girl, who was looking at Damian, lips pursed broodily. "She want to be with you."

"She can come too! The more the merrier!" Damian was enjoying this strange new high – the feeling of being drunk, but not being drunk! And things were turning out better than he could have wanted. He had found the girl – and everything was sorted! Now he was in Soi Cowboy with *two* sexy girls! *Wait till he told the guys about this!*

"You pay bar fine for girl. Six hundred baht. OK?" Nok said.

Damian shrugged. "Yeah! Whatever!"

The girl introduced as Mai squeezed his crutch appreciatively.

So it was that Damian staggered out of the Shark with a girl on each arm, a grin on his face and a pleasant warmness in his shorts …

9 - Entrapment

The Soi was still crowded with the plethora of smiling, laughing faces lost to a night of decadence and debauchery, thoughtless of responsibility or consequence, now blind devotees, even if but for this one night, to their new religion of neon goddesses. The humdrum grittiness of reality had become temporarily eclipsed by this new psychedelic fantasy. Damian was one of those faces. Everything was now how he had dared to imagine it would be – the ultimate antidote to a life of meaningless mediocrity. He embraced the intoxicating sights, sounds and smells in an almost primal way.

The girls were at a street vendor, enjoying some fried chicken. Damian joined them and Nok placed a lump of the juicy meat in his mouth. He chewed with relish and smiled at his newfound girlfriend. She pulled his arm and he found himself in front of the Moonshine Joint.

This was a place Damian was unfamiliar with, but it looked interesting enough and he allowed the girls to sit him down on a low stool by a metal table. The bar girls here wore green tops with a bare midriff, below which were white hot pants with black silver-studded belts and black high-heeled shoes. One of them brought him a beer and cocktails for the girls, along with a small metal bucket of ice.

Mai was beside him and gripped his arm, pointing at the beer. "Beer Chang!"

"Great!" Damian enthused.

She used a pair of tongs from the bucket to drop the rounded ice cubes into his tall beer glass. He looked up at the big girl. She was wearing a yellow sarong over her bikini outfit, but her deep cleavage was still clearly visible as she bent over him. He picked up the beer. "Cheers!" he said.

"In Thailand, we say, *chon gaew*!" Nok, who was sitting opposite, corrected him, lifting up her own drink.

Damian clumsily repeated the salutation and the girls giggled as they clinked glasses with him. The beer tasted as good as before and he found the coolness of the ice pleasant in this dry, humid environment.

He looked around the bar. It was certainly smaller than the others he had been to, although there was a wooden panelled door evident, which must lead into the interior. But nothing particularly special, except, perhaps, a good view of the sexy girls from the larger bars parading themselves outside. The other western patrons of the bar looked to Damian like old ex-pat men out for a night-time grope while watching the

A Bangkok Fairy Tale

obligatory football on the widescreen TVs. An older smartly dressed woman was smiling at him.

"She *mamasan* – take care of girls," Nok explained.

The woman raised her glass to Damian, as did a couple of the other girls. He raised his glass back, and then it occurred to him that he was most likely paying for their drinks, as well. He was about to say something when the *mamasan* came over to his table.

"Hello. Please to meet you," she said in a high, sing-song voice. "What is your name?"

"Eh, Damian …" Damian began.

"She very good," the *mamasan* said, gesturing to another girl in a black sarong, who had suddenly appeared by her side.

The girl did not look anything special, if she was a girl at all. She looked at least forty, with a freckled face and flat nose above which the tired, reddened eyes regarded Damian with a hint of expectation.

"She take care of you now," continued the *mamasan*, as if some sort of pre-arranged business agreement was transpiring between them.

"I'm sorry," said Damian slowly, careful to make these women understand, "but I'm with these two girls." He pointed towards Nok and Mai.

"It OK," Nok said. "You go. Not take long. We stay here."

"Why would I …?"

Nok raised a forefinger and pushed the tip in and out of her pursed lips.

"Oh–h–h!" Damian replied slowly, as the realization of the sort of service being offered dawned on him.

The girls laughed and the woman in black smiled shyly.

Damian suspiciously pondered this unexpected development. He had to admit there was something raw and earthy about this woman that somehow excited him. *But why?!* She would not normally be his type, but now the prospect of having sex with this older, not particularly attractive woman just seemed so … *damn exhilarating! What was going on?! What had Bangkok done to him?!* "You … will wait for me here?" he said to Nok, wanting to be sure that this would indeed be the case.

"Yes. We stay here," Nok reassured him."You go. She very good. I know."

Damian gave an embarrassed smile and reluctantly accepted the fact that the curiosity of being with this woman and the warm, yearning feeling from deep within the region of his shorts had gotten the better of him. "OK … what the hell!"

He allowed the woman to lead him towards the wood panelled door. Glancing back, he saw Nok and Mai in animated conversation with the *mamasan. What were they saying?* The woman opened the door for him, and he walked through into the bar's darkened interior.

There was a small dimly lit dance floor in the middle on which two black bikini-clad girls were moving lethargically to the pulsating, repetitive drone of house music. They looked older and less attractive than their contemporaries in the Shark or Baccara. Damian could make out the figures of men and girls together in the top rows of seats, shadows masking whatever unpalatable activities they may be indulging.

The woman sat Damian down on one of the other sofa seats at the back. She slid off her black sarong, and he could just make out an outline of bony arms and sagging breasts in the darkness. Her character seemed to have changed now that she had him on his own. She was no longer the quiet and shy woman he had seen on the outside, but excited and direct as she began to finger his fly and jabber something in Thai. Before Damian could have any second thoughts about what the hell he was doing here with her, she expertly had his shorts and pants round his ankles and his knees apart. Her eyes were alive and she licked her lips salaciously as she squeezed him.

"Ow! Careful!" he said, but, nevertheless, did nothing to resist. He could feel his heart beating faster – the seediness and depravity of this environment was making him more aroused; his strange state of mind making him more carefree.

The woman released him and found the room to kneel in front of his seat, her dark eyes darting pruriently as she examined his exposed lower body. Damian felt he should be embarrassed, even a touch humiliated, but was not. He did, however, feel uncomfortable as he was pushed backwards, his neck cramping awkwardly against the back seat. He tried to shift himself into a better position and lay back, submitting himself to the carnal whims of this wild lecherous woman.

Damian looked at her enthusiastically bobbing head, not entirely sure what she was doing down there … but it felt nice … *very nice!* He gasped, his fingernails digging into the soft material of the seat as he realized he could no longer contain himself and was sure he saw lights as he finally exploded with a loud sigh. The woman, however, continued to voraciously lick and suck at him as if reluctant to release her newly acquired prize so soon, and he was surprised to find himself quickly back in an aroused state, and was even more surprised as, within minutes, a second wave of ecstasy flooded over him. *That had never happened before! Damn! Nok was right! She was good!*

Damian collapsed onto his seat, breathing heavily. He looked up to see the woman grinning at him, dribble trickling out the corner of her mouth. "Th–thanks!" was all he could say.

He pushed himself upright, trying to catch his breath. Another girl came over to them carrying a silver tray with a slip of paper on. She switched on a torch, so he could see properly. It was a receipt.

"You waste no time!" he said to the girl.

Damian scanned through the tally, finding it hard to keep his eyes focused. *"Holy crap!"* he gasped. It seemed he was owing almost a hundred pounds. "This can't be right!"

The older woman edged in next to him and ran a nicotine stained finger over the pencil scratches. "This for drinks ..." she started.

"That's a helluva lot of drinks!" Damian pointed out, wincing.

"... And this for girls ... and this for me."

It seemed that he was paying for Nok and Mai, as well as this woman. *Shit!* Nevertheless, his post-orgasmic mood state mellowed the shock. *It was worth it ...! Wasn't it?*

"I'll need to use the ATM," he said.

"I come with you," the woman replied.

She guided Damian back through the wooden door, and he was not completely surprised to find his table outside vacant, but for his half-drunk glass of beer.

"They go next door. Suzie Wong. They have show. You like, sure," said the *mamasan*.

Damian flinched. *More money!*

The woman, whose rapacious animal wiles had so successfully entrapped Damian, was quiet again as she stood at a discreet distance while he punched out his PIN into a nearby ATM. He made sure to take out enough money to, hopefully, cover the rest of the evening. The crowds were beginning to thin by the time he returned to the Moonshine Joint and paid the *mamasan*.

"Five hundred baht for her," the *mamasan* said, nodding towards the woman in black.

"What?" said Damian, exasperated. "I've already paid …" The women were scowling at him, the *mamasan* holding out her hand to reinforce her point. He did not particularly want to cause any ill feelings from these people. "Never mind," he conceded.

He palmed out another five hundred baht note to the *mamasan*, who lifted her hands together gratefully in a Buddhist *wai*. With a fixed smile, Damian waved his goodbyes to the women and the girls, and walked over to Suzie Wong, which was just on the left past Jungle Jim's, a similar bar to the Moonshine Joint. Again, he found himself on a search for the enigmatic Nok …

10 - Perseverance

The Suzie Wong go-go bar was a character unto itself insofar that it was like no other bar on Soi Cowboy. There was a distinct feel of the Orient with which the patterns on the walls and glass panels were designed. Red neon blazed forth the bar's name in Oriental-style western letters enough times for any man to have no doubt where exactly he was. Above a row of electric crimson arches stood the striking mauve embodiment of the fictional Hong Kong prostitute Suzie Wong herself, pouting and proud with hand on hip, fan extended.

As Damian walked purposefully towards the main entrance, a girl in white bikini waved a sign in front of him, declaring boldly in blue and red:

A Bangkok Fairy Tale

Welcome To

SUZIE WONG

Live Shows Inside

He brushed past the girl, and a wooden door was opened for him beneath an array of red and gold Chinese lanterns. The interior was more fancifully lighted than the other bars he had been to and the Oriental theme continued with copies of traditional Chinese paintings adorning decorative pillars. The six dancing girls on the central stage were wearing fishnet stockings with little else.

Damian was ushered to a seat near the stage by a waitress and ordered another Chang beer. He was about to look around for Nok and Mai when the lights dimmed. The dancers were replaced by a solitary girl in a black kimono, illuminated by a single spotlight. Deep Purple's 'Smoke on the Water' began to play as the girl dropped the kimono revealing her nudity beneath.

The girl did not look particularly attractive to Damian – her body seemed too pale and emaciated. She produced a packet of cigarettes from somewhere and lit one up. A stool was placed behind her onto which she sat. She opened her legs and proceeded to insert the cigarette between them and … *began to smoke it!* Damian watched in morbid fascination as she continued to, somehow, puff out white wispy halos.

"That's one sure way to avoid lung cancer!" an American voice hooted from behind him.

One of the ubiquitous Japanese men reached out over the stage and lit his own cigarette from the girl's to whoops of delighted amusement from his friends.

"Damian! Damian Shoo!" a girl's voice called out.

Damian looked round and could just make out Nok and Mai sitting further back to his left. A strange sense of relief came over him and he got up to join them. He edged himself between the two of them, and Mai put her hand back on his crutch. She looked half-cut.

"You enjoy lady?" Nok asked.

"Yeah, thanks. You were right about her!" Damian replied, finishing off his beer with a contented sigh. He was certainly feeling happy with himself. Nothing like this had ever happened to him before. He was having all these different sex experiences – most of them good – just in one night. *And he was still high and horny – without being particularly plastered!*

A waitress came round with another tray of drinks. Nok picked up the paper receipt, and Damian winced again. *Just as well he had gone to that ATM!*

Another act had started on the stage. This time it was three nude girls, who were rubbing oil onto one another to some up-tempo rock music. Mai deftly unbuttoned Damian's shorts and began to caress him. One of the girls was now lying down on the stage, while the second squatted on her face, and the third knelt and licked between her legs. Damian sat back and beamed, enjoying the lesbian action on the stage and Mai's soft touch.

"Very good? Yes?" Nok said, raising her voice above the loud music.

"Oh yes!" Damian fervently agreed.

"How you feeling?"

"I've never felt better!" Damian replied, grinning at her.

Nok looked satisfied.

A Bangkok Fairy Tale

Damian looked back at the girls on the stage. He found them much sexier and more attractive than the girls before them, and, furthermore, they seemed to be genuinely enjoying themselves. They were now up on their knees, kissing, licking and probing each other and themselves with their fingers. Mai was doing some probing of her own, and then Nok's hand joined hers, gently pinching and squeezing him. Damian glanced at her. The dim contours of her exotic face were expressionless as she watched the stage show. One of the girls was bent over, another licking between the cheeks of her pert backside. Damian let out a sharp breath as Nok and Mai began to explore further into his boxer shorts. Suddenly feeling exposed, Damian quickly glanced around – all eyes seemed glued to the show – but he realized he could no longer care if anyone saw him. The third girl was inserting her fingers into the girl who was bent over, and then sucking them with relish. Just as, once again, Damian felt he could no longer contain himself, the show stopped and all went dark …

11 - Reality

As the early morning hours advanced, Soi Cowboy began to close, like a gluttonous nocturnal predator that slinks away with belly full to hide its ungainly ugliness from prying daylight eyes and sleep again until the new eve of feasting inevitably arrives. Dwindling crowds were drifting like disoriented spirits in search of whatever disparate life they had fleetingly released themselves. The finality of the evening was echoed by the clanking and grinding of metal shutters and doors, locking away the sinful guilty secrets of another Bangkok night.

Some of the bars remained open to accommodate the late night revellers for whom there was no tomorrow of consequence. Country Road was one such bar, and Damian, arms linked with his two exotic escorts, found himself seemingly floating in that direction. Despite his strangely euphoric state of mind, he felt a sudden coldness creep over him as shadowy memories – now seeming to come from an entirely different life – were relit. Instinctively, he veered himself and his companions right, towards the neon monstrosity that was the Tilac Bar, which, evidently, was also refusing to relinquish its vibrant soul to the encroaching darkness.

Fortunately, Nok and Mai did not seem to mind Damian's choice of venue and began to chat exuberantly to the girls in the outside bar area. He got himself a beer and looked out onto the darkening Soi. Three drunk western men in matching Beer Singha T-shirts were staggering past, arms around one another. Damian smiled. He did not feel particularly inebriated, or even tired. He looked back to the girls. They were gone again.

Damian felt that odd sense of unease he had experienced at the Moonshine Joint. He did not like being left on his own. *Was he to spend all his time in Thailand chasing after this one girl – whom he hardly even knew?!*

A few girls were loitering outside the bar – but not Nok or Mai. He went through the open doors into the interior of the Tilac Bar. The place was big – as big as the Baccara, if not bigger – though the size was enhanced by a strange emptiness which seemed unnatural without the girls gyrating themselves on the large central stage. A couple of women were sweeping up the floor, but, again, no sign of his elusive quarries.

"Sir …! Sir …!" a girl's voice called.

Damian turned and recognized one of the bar girls Nok and Mai had been talking to outside.

"This for you!" She handed him a crumpled piece of paper.

Damian looked at the girl suspiciously, who simply smiled back. He took the piece of paper and straightened it out. Beneath an imprint of lips in red lipstick was scrawled in pencil:

__I work in Crazy House next 3 nites__
__Sukhumvit Soi 23__
__Near Soi Cowboy__
__Come see me there!__
__Nok X__

Somewhat perplexed, Damian re-crumpled the piece of paper and stuffed it into his pocket.

"Lady like you, yes?" the girl suggested, helpfully.

"I … hope so," Damian pensively replied. *Dammit! So much for an amorous end to the evening with those two sexy girls!*

Feeling numb, he thanked the messenger girl and wandered out of the bar and back into the darkness. Lights were still on in Country Road. *Maybe the girls were there!* Well. He still was not going to go back in that place for the time being. If Nok wanted to see him at this Crazy House – a bar he had never heard of, if it was a bar – then so be it.

After wandering for a short while lost in thought, Damian found himself on Soi Asoke, where the taxi had deposited him on his first visit to Soi Cowboy. It seemed such a long time ago now, but it was just … Damian felt he was losing track of time. He looked at his Rolex, the illuminated face telling him it was just after three on Sunday the fifteenth. Damian had arrived on the thirteenth. *Shit! Just two days!* He looked around. Even now, there was traffic on the road, and he noticed there were open-air bars along the pavement, looking reassuringly open. *He could do with another drink ... and – bizarrely enough – another woman!*

He went over to the nearest bar, sat on a stool, and ordered a Jack Daniels and Coke with ice from the toothy male bartender. There were still a number of people milling around: late night revellers, taxi drivers, bar girls and staff from Soi Cowboy just finishing work. A couple of older Thai women were looking at Damian. He gave them a smile and a wink, and they giggled.

A slim, attractive girl came over and sat beside Damian. *Hello. Maybe his luck was still in!* "Can I get you a drink?" he asked her, and realized she looked strangely familiar.

The girl looked at him uncertainly. "OK. I have same as you."

"Another JD and Coke with ice," Damian said to the bartender.

The girl took the drink and quietly sipped it. She seemed unusually reticent for a Bangkok girl, Damian thought. But, she did not look like all the rest of the girls he had seen in Soi Cowboy. She was smartly dressed in a blue blouse and black skirt. Her hair was tied back, and her earrings glinted gold. She was looking different, but, smelling the alluring scent of jasmine, Damian suddenly realized who she was.

"You're the nurse from the Bangkok Hospital, aren't you?" he said, feeling a sharp tinge of exhilaration at this somewhat unexpected circumstance of seeing another sexy girl whom he knew.

Despite Damian's rather excited reaction to her presence, the girl remained calmly demure. "Yes. How are you?"

"I'm well, thanks. It's nice to see you again! My name is Damian, by the way."

She gently took his hand. "I remember. My name is Mali."

"Ma-*li*," Damian repeated, not wanting to forget. "Nice name." He found himself looking at the firm, pert outline of her breasts beneath the flimsy blouse. "So, Mali – what's a nice girl like you doing in a place like this?" He then winced at the cheesy chat-up line.

Mali, nevertheless, gave him a shy smile. "I help out in the family pharmacy shop near Soi Cowboy, as well as working in the hospital."

"I see. So … late night, huh?" Damian said, knocking back his drink.

There was an awkward silence, and then Mali suddenly looked at him, her dark, almond eyes searching. "I know what is wrong with you!"

This comment caught Damian off guard. "I'm sorry …? What?"

She put her mouth to his ear, and whispered: "You have been drugged!"

Damian froze. "What do you mean?" he whispered back, slowly.

"Look." Mali took out a compact mirror from her mauve shoulder bag, and put it to his face.

Damian did so. He looked fine. In fact, considerably well, taking into account his night on the town. Then he saw his eyes. There was something wrong. Yes. His pupils were really dilated.

"How is your head?" Mali asked.

He raised his hand to the bump on his head. *It was gone!* *"What the hell?!"* he gasped. *"There's nothing there!"*

A Bangkok Fairy Tale

Damian glanced self-consciously about the bar. Everyone was still going about their own business. The older women were chatting. The bartender was serving another customer. A group of off-shift bar girls were laughing together.

He looked back at Mali. "What happened to me?" he said, still keeping a low voice.

"Don't you see? Those girls. They use you. I saw you earlier, and I was going to come over and say hello, but then I saw … them … with you," she replied, urgently. "You are … How you say in English …? Guinea pig!"

"Guinea pig?!" Damian blurted, and then coughed – again, not wanting to draw attention to himself.

"They look for men like you," Mali continued. A sadness had crept into those dark eyes.

"What do you mean, *men like me*?" Damian hissed.

She looked away.

"Well?"

Mali looked uncomfortable as she spoke. "They have girls who look around the bars to find men … who are right … for the drugs."

"Who are *they*, and what drugs?" Damian pursued, and, as an afterthought: "And why am *I* right for the drugs?"

"I already say too much!" Mali said, looking around, as if she was afraid of being watched.

Damian was confused … and hurt. *Nok and Mai were just using him?! If those were even their real names! He needed to know more from this nurse!* He took out the crumpled note and showed it to her. "And what does this mean?"

Mali looked. Her expression changed to that of fear, as she put her hand up to her mouth. "Oh no … no …!" she gasped.

She looked up at Damian, her eyes now urgent ... desperate. "You not go there! You must leave Thailand! Now!"

Damian grabbed her wrist. "I don't know who you are or what this is all about, but I'm not going anywhere, until you tell me everything!"

"Ow! You are hurting me!"

If Damian had not wanted attention before, he certainly had it now. All eyes were on him. He released the girl. "Sorry. But I need to know what this is all about."

Mali's seemingly serene and intelligent demeanour had all but vanished, and she rubbed her wrist, pouting like a hurt child.

"Please," Damian pushed, imploringly. "You're the only one who can help me!"

Mali looked uncertain. Her solemn eyes flicked back up at Damian. "OK. We must go somewhere quiet!"

Damian quickly paid his bill and followed Mali from the bar, leaving behind a sea of curious looks. As she walked in front of him away from Soi Cowboy, Damian could not help but look – despite all the disturbing things he had just heard – at the rhythmic movement of her cute little backside. *Damn! Must be the drugs!*

It occurred to Damian that this long night – probably the longest in his life – had still not come to an end ...

12 - Metamorphosis

Mali led a bewildered Damian down a shadowy side street to one of the numerous small karaoke bars dotted about the city. The place was quiet save for a few moustached Thai men playing cards and drinking whisky at a corner table. The only illumination seemed to come from the flickering image of a Thai girl on the karaoke machine quietly singing about her broken heart. They sat at a table by the machine, and Mali waved to a large woman in an apron and said something in Thai. The woman promptly brought over a small bottle of Sangsom whisky and placed it firmly on the flowery plastic tablecloth. She came back with two tall glasses of ice and poured the whisky into them, giving Damian a smile. Damian looked around, taking in the dark, dishevelled bar, white geckos crawling up its neglected walls. He jumped slightly as a rat scuttled across the cracked tiled floor. No one else took any notice.

"We can talk here," Mali said, those dark, intelligent eyes again watching him searchingly. "How do you feel now?"

Damian still felt good, despite having lost his Thai female entourage. In fact, more than good. Despite that overhanging threat of imminent danger – which, actually, was a thrill in itself – he was tingling with excitement and continued to have that pleasant swimming feeling similar to being drunk, but without the tiredness and lack of coordination. He had had a fantastic evening, and now he was in a real Bangkok karaoke bar with another beautiful girl. *And he still felt really horny!* He began to entertain thoughts of what he wanted to do to his exotic companion, but her gaze brought him back into focus. "I feel great!" he replied, taking a draught of the smooth, cool whisky. "In fact, I don't think I can remember the last time I felt this good!"

"It is the drug. You not get drunk, you just want to drink more – and pay more money," Mali explained, patiently.

Damian thought about this. "That doesn't sound too bad. Finally – a cure for the bad effects of being drunk! And what about the nasty lump I had on my head?" he reminded her, touching the top of his forehead. "It's totally gone!"

"It makes your body work fast and want more of … everything. Then you need more drug. And then …" Mali dropped her eyes in sadness.

"And then … what?" Damian prompted, pretty sure her sentence was not going to end well.

Mali shrugged. "You die," she replied, simply.

Damian winced. *Thought so!* He felt he should be more alarmed than he actually was. "Die?" he repeated.

A Bangkok Fairy Tale

"I know of people who die."

Damian took another swig of the whisky, his blurred mind trying to make sense of what this girl was saying to him. "So ... like ... I'm going to wake up dead, or something?"

Mali's eyes were serious, but she gave a wry smile. "I hope not today."

"Great ...! So ... what do I do next?"

"I already tell you! You have to go back to England ... Before it is too late!"

Damian could see the imploring urgency in her face. It was all too much to take in. He needed some space to think. "Right. Where's the toilet here?"

Mali sighed, clearly irritated at Damian's seeming inability to grasp the seriousness of his situation. She gestured towards the back of the bar. "Round there."

He got to his feet. "Look. I appreciate you helping me, but this is a helluva lot to take in. Just give me a chance to get my head round it all." Then, as an afterthought, remembering Nok and Mai: "You'll be here when I get back. Right?"

Mai gave him a tight smile. "Yes. I not leave you. Just do not be long time."

"OK."

Damian went through a doorway from which hung strips of plastic curtain. The toilet had no gender partition, and was simply a hole in the cement floor. He smirked. *No towel guy here!* He stood over the hole and unbuttoned his shorts. Strange. He seemed to have a problem down there. Even though the shorts were quite baggy, he seemed to have difficulty ... *Jesus!* He pulled out his male appendage ... His extraordinarily *large* male appendage! He took a sharp intake of breath, hearing his heart pounding in his ears. *What the ...?!*

It must be the drugs! Not only was he more sexually aware than normal, but ... *it* had grown! He took a few more deep breaths, coughing on the rank smell of urine. His mind was whirling at this new incredible development. But ... OK. He could cope with this. It was just a bit bigger ... not freakish looking. Yeah. No worries. In fact, he could get used to it! Maybe he could become a porn star, or something!

But, that was not all that had changed. Damian was feeling a new, unfamiliar tautness about his body. He ran his fingers up the inside of his T-shirt. Any softness had gone. His stomach was flatter, more rigid. He also noticed that the muscles of his arms and legs were more pronounced than usual. *Wow! He knew the Thai food was healthy, but ...!*

"Damian? You OK?"

Mali! What was he going to tell her? Maybe he should show her his new manliness! He found that prospect quite exciting, but probably not a good idea. She might freak out ... and he needed her cool! "Just coming," he called back.

Damian was able to urinate OK, and he found his new largeness pleasantly sensitive to the touch. He felt the urge to go and find another bar girl ... but, he had to try and control himself and not let the drugs – or whatever was happening to him – take over.

He sat back down at the table, self-consciously crossing his legs. Mali was looking at him, concerned. "I need to know more," Damian said, firmly. "Like, how come you know so much?"

"My father is a policeman," Mali explained, beginning to toy with the ice in her drink. "He sees what goes on, but has no ... How you say ...? Proof!"

"He knows who's behind this?"

"They are businessmen from other countries. They are very smart … very dangerous. They have a name."

"What name?"

Despite having convinced Damian they were in a safe place, Mali glanced about nervously. She leant towards him, her brow furrowed as she tried to pronounce the word. "Sin-dee-cut."

"Syndicate!" Damian repeated.

Mali looked panicky. "*Shhh!* Do not say out loud. Even here!"

"What do they care?" he said, gesturing at the half-asleep Thai men.

"You can never be sure who *they* are!" Mali replied, coldly.

Damian took a sip from his whisky. "But … we're getting somewhere. Good!"

"I think I tell you too much."

"No. If this affects me. I need to know."

The large aproned woman returned with two small white china cups of black coffee. A small, timid girl behind her carried a plate of strips of fried meat and a pot of dark sauce with green chilli bits in.

"You must eat," Mali said.

Damian was not particularly hungry, but did as he was told. He picked up one of the strips of meat and dipped it unsparingly in the sauce.

"Careful. Spicy," Mali warned.

He spluttered, and she handed him a glass of water. "*Prik nam pla.* Fish sauce and chilli," she explained.

"Right," Damian said, his eyes watering.

"So. What you do now?" Mali asked, getting back on the subject.

Damian poured the remainder of the whisky in his coffee. "I intend to get to the bottom of this."

Mali looked at him quizzically.

"I'm going to this Crazy House."

Again, Mali looked around nervously. "Are you crazy? They will kill you!"

"Yeah. I'm gonna go crazy in the Crazy House!" He sniggered, childishly.

Mali looked at him incredulously.

"Look. They're not going to harm me if I'm their ... guinea pig. And ... the drug's already changed me."

"The drug will wear off."

"I don't think so." Damian sighed. *What the hell!* He glanced around to make sure everyone was minding their own business, and then, before Mali could react, unbuttoned his shorts. "Look!"

Wide-eyed, Mali saw the flat stomach and large ... "Oh my god!" She put her hand to her mouth.

Damian glanced around again, and quickly concealed himself. "See! What am I supposed to do about *that*?"

Mali looked momentarily shaken, and then, to Damian's utmost surprise, laughed.

"You ... find that funny?"

Mali cleared her throat. "Sorry. A bit." She clocked Damian's hurt expression. "You not like?"

"Well. I guess it's a deformity I can learn to live with. But, it's going to make me a bit self-conscious when I return to the UK."

"I think you will go back as you were – again, when drug wears off. But, I know a doctor, a friend of my father." Mali scowled. "I think you are like donkey – you not listen, you stay in Thailand. So, I take you to see her."

"Donkey? You mean stubborn? Well … I'm certainly hung like one now!" Damian sniggered again at his own joke, but Mali just looked blank. He gave an embarrassed cough. "So … you're going to help me …? Right?"

Was that a smile he detected? "I think you are a foolish man … but I will help you. And you will help my father to stop these people."

Damian was satisfied with this reply. In fact, he now felt like a secret agent! *He was James Bond 007 … agent to thrill and shock … complete with his big …*

"Damian!"

Damian realized he was giggling stupidly to himself. "What? Yes?"

Mali looked at him with an air of suspicion. "I think you need to get some rest. The drug and alcohol together are making you crazy. You have a phone?"

"It's in my hotel."

Mali went to the bar and returned with a piece of paper with her phone number scribbled on it. "Call me."

"Can't I come back with you?" Damian asked, hopefully.

"I do not think that is a good idea. You need to sleep. Drink plenty of water. Wait for drug to wear off."

Damian sighed disappointedly, but he could see her point.

Mali touched his arm, a look of concern returning to those alluring eyes. "This is not going to be easy."

Damian smiled back. "As long as I'm with you, I'll be OK."

"Now you go back to hotel."

Mali got to her feet, lightly brushing her hand on his shoulder before being swallowed up into the encroaching daylight. Damian sighed again. His mind was still spinning. He had been launched from a world of abject innocuousness into one of the absolute and complete opposite. Too much was happening at once, but, if nothing else, this new, weird drug, which was probably killing him, was, also, strangely helping him to cope. He looked appreciatively at the buxom serving lady, and ordered himself another whisky …

13 - Intoxication

A seething sea of exotic brown feminine forms stretching out as far as the eye could see beneath a scarlet Bangkok sky half-shrouded by towering distorted skyscrapers and angry dark, rolling clouds. The bodies writhed and intertwined, moaning and luxuriating in their own unspeakable carnal sin. Faster and faster they moved until they engulfed and merged into one another to form an undulating blanket of seamless prurient flesh.

A clap of thunder ...

Damian woke to the knocking on the door. He jerked upright into a sitting position, the blanket slipping off, revealing his new nakedness. *Jesus! It had really happened!* He looked around blearily. At least he was safely back in his hotel room, although he did not remember returning. *How long had he been sleeping?!*

The knocking resumed. Damian tried to get his thoughts together. He felt fine, except for a particularly dry throat. He wrapped himself in a towel and went to open the door, picking up and drinking a half-empty bottle of Coke from the floor on the way. The cleaning lady stood outside with her trolley.

"Err. Come inside," Damian said, rubbing the sleep from his eyes.

The cleaning lady looked disapprovingly at Damian and his dishevelled room, and then went about her business. Damian winced at the sunlight streaming through the window and went to the bathroom to splash cold water onto his face. He looked in the mirror. He was unshaven and … his pupils were still a bit dilated. *But, what day was this?*

On his bedside table were crumpled pieces of paper and baht notes, along with coins and his cheap Rolex. He grabbed the watch, looking for the date display. *Monday 16th – 12.34 p.m. He had missed a day!* He opened the pieces of notepaper … Mali's phone number … Nok's message about the Crazy House … *He had another couple of nights, if he was going to see her there!*

The cleaning lady was talking to him about something he could not understand. He felt a wave of irritation, and then a wicked thought struck him. He dropped his towel.

"You want some of this?" he said, pointing at his newly developed assets.

She stopped talking in mid-sentence, eyes widening, aghast. Before Damian could say anything more, she was out the door, trolley rattling behind.

Damian could not help but giggle manically to himself. He wanted to get rid of her, but ... he was half-hoping she would stay. *He would have quite liked to have got his hands on that plump little body!* Damian checked himself, and felt a cold feeling of embarrassment slowly creep over him. The embarrassment edged into panic. *That bloody drug was still affecting his thoughts and behaviour!* He had to call Mali ... see this doctor she was talking about ... but his phone was in the reception deposit box. He felt he should have a warm shower and relieve himself – get the dirtiness out of his mind. But, he felt an overwhelming sense of urgency and nervous energy that was pushing him onwards ... and he had a strong desire to see Mali again ... and Nok ...!

14 – Alliance

The taxi was jammed within the midst of midday Bangkok traffic in a heat that would fray the temper of many a western city commuter. But the Thais typically took it all in their stride, quite content to quietly adopt their national Buddhist-inspired philosophy of *mae pen rai* – 'never mind – whatever will be, will be'. Damian's driver had his elbow out the window, patiently wearing that usual expression of street weary resignedness upon his craggy, sweat-beaded face, as he jerked his car to a halt once more and waved on a teenage motorcyclist with scowling girlfriend riding side-saddle behind.

Damian, too, had little interest in these extraneous irritations, but for different reasons. He had far more serious problems on his mind. After picking up his phone from the reception desk, he had exited the Udomsuk Hotel somewhat rapidly, too embarrassed to look anyone in the eye, after the painfully toe-curling incident with his cleaning lady. He had then jumped on the nearest taxi for Soi Cowboy, and was now flicking through the missed call senders and text messages. The latest text was sent that morning by Jason, and he did not seem too happy.

> Where the f*** are you?!
> Did you find that b****?!
> The guys think UR a f***ing hero!!
> I think UR a f***ing t***!!
> Call me!!

Damian, however, could not particularly care – he now felt strangely detached from his life back in the UK. The only person he had any desire to call right now was Mali. He stabbed out her number and put the phone to his ear. There was a dial tone. He heard a female voice speak Thai. It must be her. He felt his heart quickening. "It's me. Damian."

A pause.

"Hello?" Damian persevered, feeling his throat go dry.

"Where are you?"

Damian exhaled, feeling a sense of relief at her response. "I'm in a taxi, heading for Soi Cowboy."

Another pause. "Damian, I am busy right now." He could hear voices in the background. "I call you back."

She was gone. Damian stared at the battered Nokia in frustration. Two minutes later the ring tone came on. He quickly snapped the phone to his ear. "Hello!"

"Are you all right?"

"The drug's still affecting me. Where can I meet you?"

"Name a safe place you know."

Damian thought for a moment. For some reason, the English-themed pub he had visited popped into his head. Maybe he felt safer in a more homely atmosphere. And ... being on the corner of Sukhumvit Soi 23 and Soi Cowboy ... it must be close to where the Crazy House was! "That English pub on Sukhumvit Soi 23."

"I know. It is near where I work. I wait for you there. Then we see doctor."

She hung up again. Damian gave a self-satisfied smile. Talking to Mali again made him feel more secure, as if reaffirming all he had been through. And, if this doctor could help him, all the better. *But, what was to happen then?* He had definitely made his mind up to go to this Crazy House in the evening, whatever Mali or anyone else said.

"Soi Cowboy," the taxi driver announced, and pointed out the window.

Damian looked. It all seemed so different, so innocuous in the day-time. Conveniently, he was at the Sukhumvit Soi 23 end again, and he did not have to walk the full length of Soi Cowboy, and past Country Road.

He paid the driver the cheaper day-time rate, and ran across the road, easily finding the Ship Inn. Once within the coolness of the pub Damian looked around, feeling more relaxed at seeing a few westerners hanging about the bar – and there was Mali sitting – strangely enough – at the same table he had sat. She was looking as smart and beautiful as he had remembered, and drinking a cola. Damian got himself a Chang.

"A bit early for beer," Mali commented, but gave him that engaging Thai smile.

Damian looked at his watch, as he sat next to her. "It's past three."

She studied his face. "You look better than last time."

"Thanks." He took a sip of the chilled beer, and grinned at her. "I'm still feeling horny, though."

Mali put a hand to her mouth to suppress a laugh. "Next time, you be careful what girl you talk to, and what she put in your drink."

Damian was glad she now seemed in better humour concerning this bizarre situation. "I'm happy with the girl I'm talking to now."

Mali glanced down at her drink, betraying a tinge of embarrassment.

Damian was beginning to feel there was a strong connection growing between the two of them, which made him warm inside. But, right now, there were more pressing issues to deal with. "So … I take it that this Crazy House place is near here?" he said in a low voice, remembering how Mali felt about people listening in.

Mali sighed, showing her reluctance to speak of this subject. "It is further along this road. If you still want to go there … you go tonight."

"That was my plan." Damian noticed the concern beginning to cloud her countenance again. "Hey! Lighten up! I'll be fine!" he said jovially, giving her his best boyish grin.

She raised her eyes to meet his, a glimmer of a smile forming on those full lips.

"That's more like it! So … what now? Hadn't I better see that doctor friend of yours?"

"Yes. Her name is Ursula Kamanatra. She is friend of my family, and is half Thai, half Indian. She have English husband, and her English is very good. Better than me."

"Nothing wrong with your English," Damian said, a bit too quickly. "Where can we meet her?"

But, Mali was looking away. "Who is that?"

She nodded her head towards the bar, and Damian saw the little girl before she disappeared behind the other bystanders. *Dammit! He had totally forgotten about Nok's sister! What is it about her and this place?! Maybe it was something to do with the Crazy House!*

"She … is the sister of the girl … who spiked my drinks," he informed Mali, wearily.

She scowled at him. "I thought you said this place was safe."

"My brain's not exactly working on all cylinders, right now," Damian retorted.

"We must leave," Mali said, finishing her drink.

"Where to?" enquired Damian, knocking back his beer.

"The pharmacy, where I work."

Mali was quickly up and out the door, leaving Damian to hurriedly pay for the drinks and follow. He caught up with her as she was passing the turning to Soi Cowboy. The pharmacy was on the left, just after the Soi's first bar. Its automatic door hissed open with a chime and she ushered him into the air-conditioned interior. A plump, curly haired woman was at the counter.

"This is my mother, Dao," Mali said.

Damian greeted her in Thai and she lifted her hands into a *wai* in return. Mali was on her phone, as Damian looked around his neat, trim surroundings of pharmaceutical condiments. As she spoke on the phone, Mali guided him into a back room. Within its sparsely furnished confines, Damian was taken aback to see one of the khaki-clad policemen standing in the corner.

Mali seemed to notice his unease. "It is OK. This is my father. His name is Anurak. He will help you."

The policeman silently gave Damian a polite *wai*.

"I am sorry. He not speak English," Mali explained, putting her phone away. "I will speak for him."

"Who was that you were talking to?" Damian asked.

"Ursula. She is on her way."

"Oh. Good," Damian replied, uncertainly. He was not quite sure what he had got himself into.

"Please, sit," Mali said, gesturing towards a mat on the clean, tiled floor.

Damian did so, crossing his legs and gratefully accepting a glass of whisky from Mali's father, who sat opposite with his own drink.

"My father knows about Crazy House, but does not know what goes on inside," Mali said, sitting next to Damian.

"Why can't he go and see?" Damian said.

"They will know who he is. So, that is where you can help him."

The policeman raised his glass to Damian, showing his white teeth with a grin.

"Chon gaew!" Damian said, remembering the Thai salutation and raising his glass back.

"Chon gaew!" Anurak reciprocated, and then said something aside to Mali.

"He say you speak Thai good," she told Damian.

Damian shrugged. "Not really, but thanks. So, you're now OK with me going to the Crazy House?"

"If you go, you do as we say. Then, maybe, you will be OK," Mali said with a sigh.

Damian could see that Mali was still not happy about him visiting this place. But, it was good she cared.

Mali's mother entered the room, carrying a tray of food: strips of meat, a dip and spicy vegetables. She put it down next to them.

Damian thanked her in Thai. Maybe he *was* getting the hang of this language! "What do you want me to do?" he said to Mali, picking up a piece of the meat with his fingers and, this time, making sure he was careful when he dipped it in the sauce.

"If you see anything, you take pictures," she replied. "You have … ah … camera … in your phone?"

"Yeah. Sure. But what do you mean 'see anything'? Like what?"

Mali translated for her father. He replied in his soft, quiet voice.

"Anything sus … sus … ooh!" Mali was getting frustrated with her English again.

"Suspicious," Damian finished for her.

"Yes! Sus-pish-uss! All my father knows is that very strange things go on there."

Strange things! Damian was becoming increasingly intrigued with this Crazy House, but still had no idea of what to expect or what he was supposed to be taking pictures of. "Right … but what if they try to drug me again?"

Mali repeated the question to her father, who pursed his thin lips in thought before replying.

"Make sure you not drink anything. Pretend!" Mali translated.

Her father nodded at him gravely to reinforce the point.

"OK. I can do that," Damian replied. He could always get a drink before he went Dutch courage and all that.

An attractive older woman entered the room accompanied by Mali's mother. She was carrying a small silver attaché case. Anurak respectfully got to his feet and greeted her. Mali and Damian followed suit.

"This is Ursula. The doctor I was telling you about," said Mali.

"And you must be Damian," Ursula said, looking him up and down. Her accent was almost English. "You've been through rather a lot, I gather."

"Too right!" Damian replied. "You know about this drug?"

"I need to talk to Damian alone," Ursula said to Mali, and then something aside to her parents.

"Of course," Mali said.

Mali went about gathering her family together, and they left Damian alone with the doctor. Anurak gave Damian a parting nod, raising his eyebrows and putting a thumb up. Damian was not quite sure what to make of that.

Ursula beckoned for him to sit back down on the mat. He watched with some degree of bemusement as she sat down opposite and started to unfasten the case. She was undoubtedly a handsome woman. The Indian attributes were obvious: the deep, dark eyes; the curly, raven black hair, with just a hint of grey; the fullness of her lips.

"Anurak is a brave man," she was saying. "The other police are paid to turn a blind eye to the activities of this organization …"

"The Syndicate?" Damian said, remembering what Mali had told him.

"Yes. The Syndicate is made up of faceless international businessmen and works with the *chao pho* – Thai mafia."

Damian gave a low whistle. "It's … quite a big outfit then?"

I'm sorry you got caught up in this, Damian. But you can help! If the local police know about Anurak's involvement, they will … turn on him. That is why he cannot show his face in any of their bars or clubs." Ursula suddenly looked solemn, as if picturing the unpleasant things the other police would do to Mali's father if he betrayed them. "He is such a good man. He was there for me when …" She caught herself and looked back up at Damian, her dark eyes now tearful, almost imploring. "Good people are being hurt. These … criminals … deal with drugs and human trafficking. But … with your help … we can get evidence … and go to a higher authority."

Damian was warming to the doctor … in more ways than one! He noticed she was not wearing a wedding ring. *Maybe things went wrong with her English husband … Maybe there was something more between her and Mali's father …!* He gave this now increasingly desirable woman … this now increasingly desirable and possibly available woman … his sincerest look. "Don't worry," he said. "I will help you as best I can."

Ursula took a deep breath, as if in an attempt to regain her professional composure. "Thank you, Damian. You're a sweet man." She held up a small bottle of clear liquid for him to see. "Androstonene-beta-five. Known on the street as 'jizz'. It's a synthesized anabolic steroid, but this is just a crude sample. The stuff inside you is slightly more … sophisticated."

"Do you have an antidote?" Damian asked, wanting to get the most important question about this drug out of the way.

"I need to make a few quick tests first," Ursula replied, looking back into her case.

"What kind of tests?"

"I'm not sure of the quantity in your system. It should wear off in time, if you're not a regular user. I have something which should help, but I need to make sure there is no long-term damage."

Damian remembered what Mali had said about people dying, and began to feel anxious. *But ... maybe the fact he was now feeling more concerned about his personal welfare was a good thing!* "Like what?" he pressed the doctor.

"Well. Sterility ... heart and liver problems ... memory loss ..."

"Death?"

"Yes ... eventually."

"Shit!"

Ursula put a hand lightly on his arm. There was now a hint of sympathy in those alluring eyes. "You're not a regular user, Damian," she reminded him, softly. "The Syndicate has scouts to target the right sort of person that would be most compatible for the drug's effects. Usually a male tourist on his own. So, I'm afraid you met those criteria."

Damian felt a cold chill creep over him. He remembered what Mali had said to him. "I'm the guinea pig!"

Ursula gave a sad smile. "A bit of a crude analogy, but ... yes."

Damian remembered how hurt he had felt when Mali first told him that he was the right sort of man to be targeted. It was a bit of a blight to the ego to think that those sexy girls he had met were just using him. When Mali had been evasive about the matter of why he was 'the right man' some crack had opened up in his self-belief. He had never seemed to be particularly lucky with girls, and this had bothered him. That was why his friends had egged him on in his pursuit to come to Thailand. "So, that's why I was chosen. Because I'm a stupid, naive male tourist on my own," he said, awkwardly.

Ursula's dark, intelligent eyes now seemed to be searching inside him … intoxicating him. For an instant, Damian thought he was looking at an older Mali. *Maybe …?* Any developing thoughts on Mali's true parentage trailed off as he realized Ursula had still not removed her hand from his arm and her grip had perceptibly tightened. He was now feeling an electric thrill from her touch and finding himself becoming more aware of her physicality, and could not help but look at the fullness of her breast beneath the cotton blouse that was unbuttoned just a little bit too far. There was a thin gold necklace about her throat that disappeared tantalizingly into the dip of her dark cleavage, below which the only other hint of the delights that lay within was that of the imprints of nipple pushing out against the thin fabric. His mind was muddled and for those few moments he had forgotten about any entrenched insecurity. Even the true nature of the insidious promises of gratuitous fulfilment now being whispered to his darkest desires by this new raging demon pulsating in his veins was being ignored. He wanted this woman so bad.

Ursula removed her hand from him and the connection – if there had been one – broke away. "I think you are a kind, sensitive man," she said, gently. "Those horrid people are trying to exploit that. But please remember that not all Thai are the same. It is not for no reason that Thailand has been known as 'the land of smiles', and I want you to see that."

These words, somehow, reassured Damian, and, consequently, did little to temper his mounting attraction for this beautiful, astute Asian doctor.

"Now. Back to the matter at hand. Take off your shirt and let me have a look at you," Ursula continued, seemingly and almost insanely unaware of his increasingly uncontrollable feelings.

A window of lucidity momentarily glimmered into Damian's consciousness, and he pushed himself away from her. "I ... don't think that's a good idea!" he replied, breathlessly.

Ursula only smiled. But, it was a comforting smile, suggesting that all was right; she was in control. "I've studied these types of steroid. You can trust me. All you have to do is relax."

"What about ...?" Damian nodded towards the door, thinking about Mali and her family.

"They understand. They know we need this time together."

What the hell did she mean by that?! Oh well. She's the doctor! Damian thought with that same feeling of mad resignation that had become so pleasantly familiar to him over the few days he had been in this country. He pulled off his T-shirt and let this goddess of a woman examine him. She ran her soft hands across his newly enhanced body, and his muscles tightened to the tender, exhilarating touch. *Surely she must be aware of what was lurking down there in his shorts?!*

"How does that feel?"

As if she needed to ask! "Very nice. And those muscles didn't used to be there."

"Increased sensitivity. Muscular augmentation. Typical effects of androstenene," Ursula said, half to herself.

Damian felt a bit disappointed by her distant clinical appraisal. "Are you sure that's all that's changed?" he said, prompting her.

"There would be psychological effects too. Over-confidence. Increased risk behaviour. Lowering of moral values." Ursula pondered. "And please don't be embarrassed if you're easily sexually aroused. The drug will do that to you as well."

No kidding! thought Damian. She must be ignoring the proverbial 'elephant in the room' to spare his modesty. *Well ... maybe it was time to show her the elephant's trunk! The doctor said herself that he need not be embarrassed!* "Thanks. Then, maybe you should see this!"

With the same overwhelming thrill as he had felt with Mali (and, indeed, the hotel cleaning lady) – that so easily seemed to cloud better judgement – Damian got to his feet and let all hang out!

He was satisfied that the doctor's reaction was almost identical to that of Mali's. "Oh my god!" she said, putting her hand to her mouth.

It would, in fact, seem that Ursula's professional composure had now completely fallen as she looked up wide-eyed, mouth half open at the uncompromising length dangling before her. Damian was certainly getting used to – and, indeed, enjoying! – this new sensation of exposing his nakedness to women without the usual dampening effects of being self-conscious. OK. It was the andros ... *whatever the hell it was!* ... and he could not help himself but to take full advantage of this fantastic woman's sudden vulnerability. Ursula was strangely silent but for a heavy breath as he crouched next to her savouring the moment as he slowly unbuttoned the rest of her blouse.

"Damian … wait …" she then said, her voice low, hoarse.

She was saying something about pheromones, but Damian was not listening – he was fixated. He was about to push open her blouse to unleash the fruits of his fevered desire when the pendant at the end of the gold chain dropped out, catching his attention. It was a small Buddha. Something deep inside made him stop – a distant voice of caution screaming to be heard.

"I'm … so sorry," he said, a welling of tears beginning to sting his eyes.

"It's OK. I understand," Ursula replied, her voice now soft, soothing.

She gave him a close, tight hug, and for the first time since he could remember, Damian no longer felt alone …

15 - Acceptance

"How are you feeling?"

Damian looked up. Ursula was refilling his glass from the bottle of Anurak's Mekhong whisky. She had already taken a blood sample from him and injected an initial shot of – what she hoped – was a rudimentary antidote consisting of an anti-steroid formula. Of course, he would have to receive more. "I'm feeling much better, thanks," he replied, putting his T-shirt back on.

"Considering your present resistance to the negative effects of alcohol, this can't do you much immediate harm," she said with a wry smile, handing him the drink.

Damian took a sip. He *was* feeling better. The fact that he had been able to talk about his feelings to someone who understood and cared had certainly helped. In the short time he had known her, Ursula had become his friend, his confidante. He had already told her all about his previous adventures and misadventures in this manic city – even the embarrassing encounter with his hotel cleaning lady.

"What came over me?!" he had moaned, exasperated. Obviously, it had been the drug, but Damian just could not believe he would behave in such a way whatever the circumstance.

"The androstenene. That's what came over you," Ursula had reaffirmed. "I don't think you realize just how potent it is." Seeing the look of embarrassment on Damian's face, she had put a comforting arm around his shoulders. "Please don't worry yourself, Damian. It wasn't your fault. The androstenene you were given has also been enhanced … incredibly. Hence the …" her large, dark eyes had momentarily widened "… *amazing* physical changes … but any sexual stimulus you encounter, however mild, will activate the drug's effects. And those effects will not just be experienced by you. Pheromones are released that act as a sexual stimulant on the woman that has captured your interest, as well. In this case … *me!*"

Damian had then realized why she had been muttering something about pheromones in the heat of the moment. *He was a walking sex machine!*

"And yet … despite this potency … you managed to hold back and … protect us both," she had continued, emotion creeping into her voice, her eyes glimmering with respect, even admiration.

This heartfelt comment had warmed Damian inside, but there was still that nagging fear hanging over him. "What's … going to happen to me?" he had asked, tentatively.

"Damian ... I don't know. Nothing ... for now. You will develop a physical addiction as well as more stress on your body as your metabolism increases, if you continue to use the androstenene." She must have seen the expression on his face and had smiled sympathetically. "But, it's not going to come to that. We will find a way to get that poison out of your system."

Damian had returned her smile. "I'll hold you to that."

Ursula had looked thoughtful for a moment. "And those women you associated with ..."

"Nok and Mai?"

"Yes. It sounds like they're on the female compatible form of the drug – oestronene-beta-five. Which means they're also in danger."

A feeling had stirred from within Damian. He had to protect Nok. "All the more reason why I want to help you," he had said, resolutely.

Damian finished his whisky, just as Ursula's phone chirped. She picked it out of her trouser pocket and spoke into it in Thai. "It's Mali," she said to Damian. "It's time to go."

"Where now?" Damian asked, getting to his feet.

"Why, the Crazy House, of course."

16 - Strategy

The Bangkok sky was beginning to darken once more as Damian followed Mali, Ursula and Anurak back towards Soi Cowboy. The neon lights of the bars had flickered back to life and the crowd of rowdy westerners was, again, beginning to swell. This time, though, Damian did not feel the thrill of exhilaration and anticipation. Instead, there was a cold feeling of anxiety and trepidation of what the unexpected had designed for him. He rubbed his arm, still stinging from the injections Ursula had given him. She had told him that the anti-steroids would help counter the effects of his impulsive behaviour and straighten his mind out for whatever the hell it was he was about to confront.

Before they reached the Ship Inn, however, Anurak gestured towards the adjacent Dutch styled pub directly on the corner of Soi Cowboy. It was the one Damian had noticed before on his first visit to this end of the Soi and it had the same antiquated European look to it as its neighbour, but more greenery in the form of potted plants around the entranceway, above which hung a large wooden cart wheel. On either side of this were old-fashioned wooden-looking signs showing that the pub's name was, indeed, the Old Dutch.

"We go in here first. My father does not want to go any further, in case he is seen," explained Mali.

"OK," Damian complied. That was fine by him. He could get that drink he had promised himself for Dutch courage – fortuitously enough in a Dutch bar!

The inside of the Old Dutch was similar to that of the Ship Inn in that it was cluttered with various archaic ornaments and pictures of European origin. The dim lighting emanated mainly from lamps and circular electric signs advertising Heineken and Guinness on the ceiling. There were a few people around, which was a good thing, Damian thought – it would draw less attention to them. They sat down at a table opposite the bar. Damian noticed to their left was a red pillar upon which hung gold framed monochrome photographs portraying obscure scenes from, presumably, the Netherlands.

Anurak returned from the bar with a couple of iced whiskies for himself and Damian, and a couple of similarly iced colas for the women.

Damian gratefully took his drink. *"Chon gaew!"* he said, again.

"Chon gaew!" Anurak replied, grinning at him.

Ursula joined in with the salutation, but Mali did not. She was looking away, her expression seemed distracted.

"You OK, Mali?" Damian asked.

She turned back to him, and he realized that she had become tearful, her lips trembling. "I ... I am sorry, Damian, but ... I do not want you to go to that place ... I am afraid for you!"

Anurak was looking sad, too, and he pointed at Damian's half-empty glass to silently inform him he was getting a refill, before pushing his chair aside and returning to the bar.

Ursula, however, remained calm and collected. "You are being very brave, Damian. We ... Anurak ... would not blame you at all if you change your mind."

Damian found himself deeply moved by Mali's concern. He felt strongly for her too, but he also had a need ... however misplaced and irrational it may be ... to see Nok again. He looked Mali directly in the eye. "Mali. I understand, but I need to go," he told her, gently. "Not just for Anurak ... but, for myself."

She returned his gaze, and forced a smile back.

Ursula reached out and took his hand. "We'll be there for you." Her voice was reassuring, but there was something more in those deep brown eyes. She had not forgotten the intimacy they had shared together.

Anurak returned with two more whiskies.

"*Korp kun khrap*, Anurak," Damian thanked him. "I think I'm pretty much ready for anything right now!"

It occurred to Damian that things could not, actually, be that bad, with all these gorgeous women doting after him. This would never have been the case back home. *Back home!* He suddenly remembered his neglected family and friends. He noticed a sign on the wall informing patrons that the toilet was upstairs, and excused himself from his companions.

The toilet was a dishevelled, rusty-looking bowl, but Damian was not there to make use of it. He needed some alone time in which to try and contact Jason. A text message would be best – he did not want to talk. He took a moment to compose something in his mind – something short and succinct, without giving too much away. Taking out his phone, he began to quickly type.

> Hey Jace!
> Sorry I've not been in touch, but things are happening! Big things!!
> Can you see what you can find out about an Asian drug cartel known as the Syndicate??
> I'm helping the Thai police to bust them!!
> I don't have time to tell you anymore!
> Please keep this quiet! I mean it – don't tell anyone!!
> But if you don't hear anything from me within the next week – contact the UK police!!
> Thanks pal!!

Damian squinted at the blurring message. (Ursula's antidote must be starting to counteract the drug – he was feeling the effects of alcohol!) His thumb hovered uncertainly over the tab to send. *Damn! What the hell was Jason going to make of that?!* He took a deep breath, and sent the message. *Right! Let's get on with this!*

He vacated the toilet, the wooden steps creaking beneath him as he made his way back to the bar. The others were waiting for him, expectantly.

"Are you ready?" Ursula asked.

Damian finished off his whisky. "I'm ready!"

She got to her feet and gave him a hug. Again, it was tight and pleasant. "Anurak and I will wait for you here," she said in his ear. "Mali will walk you to the Crazy House. If you have any trouble – get out fast … and you have Mali's mobile number?"

Damian nodded. "Yes. Don't worry."

Anurak clasped his arm. A look of gratitude in his reddening eyes.

"Come on," Mali said, her face serious.

They pushed through the accumulating crowd and were soon back in the humid evening air.

17 – Confrontation

A light spattering of rain had begun as Damian and Mali hurriedly walked back up Sukhumvit Soi 23. Damian was grateful for the gentle cool touch of water on his face, as he tried to focus his mind again. He glanced at the Ship Inn as they passed – no sign of Nok's sister watching them.

They continued past the car park and the road darkened. There was nothing more to be seen but grey shops shuttered up against the encroaching nightfall. The crowds of Soi Cowboy had seemingly disappeared behind them. This new silence was broken by the ring tone of Damian's phone. He grimaced. *Jason was trying to call him! Dammit!* He reached down and switched the phone off. *Now was not the right time!*

"Who was that?" Mali asked.

"It's ... not important, right now," Damian replied with an irritated sigh.

They walked on without speaking, until the beat of music could be heard. About a couple of hundred yards ahead was the dark silhouette of a building bathed in an eerie neon glow.

"The Crazy House," Mali said in a low voice, as if not wanting to be heard.

As they approached, it became evident to Damian that the building was a bar, not particularly dissimilar to any other on Soi Cowboy. But, the blazing red neon sign on the front made it quite clear that this was, indeed, his objective!

Outside, a few bikini-clad girls were loitering about or sitting at tables, chatting and eating food from a street vendor. A few motorcycles were scattered about the pavement, and a mean-looking thickset man dressed in black was standing, tattooed arms crossed, at the entrance.

"I'm gonna take a photo of the outside," Damian said to Mali, and took back out his phone.

He switched it on again. Two missed calls and a text from Jason. He was tempted to read the text, but did not want to be distracted. It might say something that would nudge his sanity and make him change his mind. He put the phone on camera mode, and made sure no one was looking in his direction before pointing it towards the bar and taking a couple of snaps.

"This is where I must leave you," Mali said.

Damian's heart dropped. "OK. I'll be as quick as I can, then see you back at that Dutch place."

"Remember. Just find out what you can. Try and see that girl you met, but be very careful of her. She is no good!"

"Right." *Was there a tinge of jealousy towards Nok?*

Mali leant towards him and kissed him on the lips. The kiss was firm and lingering. Damian caught a glimpse of her tearful, doe-like eyes before she abruptly turned and disappeared into the darkness and misty rain.

Damian took a deep breath. He felt intoxicated by her touch. His heart was pounding, his mind whirling. *Would he ever see her again?* He could still go after her … turn away from this madness. *No!* He had to get these thoughts out of his mind. This was something he had to do.

He looked back towards the Crazy House – his unforeseen destiny here in Thailand. The girls were still there, and the doorman was smoking a cigarette. *Here we go!* With a surge of adrenaline, Damian clenched his fists and strode purposefully towards the bar entrance. The rain had become heavier as he approached, but he hardly noticed. The front of the bar was decorated with illuminated stone-like murals depicting girls in an assortment of erotic positions. In the middle of this was the red curtained entranceway with a sign on the left displaying bold Thai script below which were the pictorial symbols of guns, cigarettes, cameras and mobile phones with red lines through them.

Damian surreptitiously switched his phone back off, and tried to look happy and confident as he passed the girls. They smiled at him, and he smiled back. The doorman, however, did not smile, but, to Damian's relief, simply nodded at him and pulled open the curtain. *So far, so good!*

He entered the bar to be greeted by flashing lights, blaring music and dry ice. Again, he could see no obvious difference between this place and the likes of the Shark or the Baccara. Although, it was not as crowded as these bars – maybe it was still too early in the evening. He made his way easily towards the dancing stage, the other bar clientele seeming nondescript within the dazzling fluorescence and smoky atmosphere, and then the difference was made clear to him, hitting his senses squarely and solidly.

Damian's jaw dropped. He did not need any drug to appreciate what his eyes now beheld. The girls on the large figure eight-shaped stage were like none he had ever seen before. They were pictures of female magnificence, at least ten in all – tall, statuesque, with unbelievable breasts that were both huge and pert, as if defying gravity itself. They were also quite naked.

The swirling mist of dry ice and the searchlight style of illumination scanning the dance floor created the tantalizing effect of only revealing parts of the girls at any one time as they moved slowly and luxuriantly in time to the pulsating music. Some were rubbing oil onto themselves and each other, making their milky brown bodies glisten in the ethereal ambience.

Damian moved in for a closer look, momentarily forgetting why he was there in the first place. He was now on the edge of the dance floor, looking up at these extraordinary Thai goddesses. One of them noticed him. She stooped over the stage, her breasts hanging pendulous before him. As if in a dream, Damian reached up and cradled those marvellous, fleshy mounds in his hands. *They definitely felt real – no plastic here!* It certainly did not escape his attention that these girls had been, without doubt, subjected to the female version of the body enhancement drug.

Another girl emerged from the incandescence, showing him a long, slender black-taloned finger before inserting it into the first girl from behind. She withdrew her finger and began to suck and lick it lasciviously with a pierced, snake-like tongue. Damian's new bigness was painfully pushing outwards for freedom. He was seriously thinking about opening his shorts again for the girls when a sharp, intrusive voice came into his head: *'Any sexual stimulus you encounter, however mild, will activate the drug's effects!'*

Ursula's warning! Damian backed away from the Siren-like temptation. *Whatever the antidote she had given him, it was not strong enough to cope with this!* The girl licked her luscious lips, watching him with salacious, almost hypnotic dark eyes before being re-enveloped by the luminescent mist.

Damian backed away further. His heart seemed to be pounding in time to the throbbing house music.

"Hell-ooo, Damian Shoo! You come to see me at last! I thinking you forget about me!"

He spun round ... *and there was Nok!* Damian felt a wave of happiness and relief to see her again, but there was something different about her. Her face was even more over made-up than he had remembered before, her hair done in a new way, but her body was looking more fantastic than ever in tight black bikini top and thong. "Nok! I ..." he began, but his mind went blank.

Nok gave a coy smile and waved a finger at him. "But I know you come tonight!"

Damian smiled back. "Of course!" *Her sister must have told her he was around!*

She squeezed his crutch. "I think you ready for me!"

Damian was in no position to disagree. He allowed Nok to lead him by the hand into the darker recesses of the establishment. Any rational thoughts he might have had had now been replaced by the simple driving force of raw lust and desire. *The drug seemed to be having more control over him – not less!*

He found himself on a sofa, Nok sitting next to him. She handed him a beer. *Don't drink it!* he tried to remind himself.

"Now I want to see!" Nok said, and reached for his shorts. She bared her small pearl-like teeth in an expression of uninhibited carnal hunger, making her look even more unrecognizable to Damian, as she clumsily pulled at his clothing.

A sudden surge of anger replaced Damian's bewildered lustful state as he remembered what she had done to him, and he grabbed hold of her arm. *"Why did you drug me?"* The words came out as a snarl, though he had not intended them so.

Nok pulled her hand free and stared at him. Her eyes looked addled and confused for a moment, and then there was a glint of contempt. "Because I can!"

A cold feeling came over Damian. Again, he felt hurt and used. "When ... did you start giving me ... the jizz?" He tried to keep his voice measured, controlled.

The contempt in Nok's transformed face was now leering. "We want give it to you at Country Road, but you have accident ... and then you come back!" She laughed, mocking him. "My sister tell me and I look for you. Then we give you jizz!"

Damian slumped back. *Shit! What an idiot he had been! If he hadn't come back looking for Nok, he wouldn't have been poisoned! It was his pathetic need ... his obsessive desire ... to see her again that had got him into this trouble! They must have spiked his beer at ... the Shark ... the Moonshine Joint ... Suzie Wong ... Oh god! That's what they must have been jabbering on about to the* mamasan *at the Moonshine Joint!*

They were all in on it! The anger and hurt were now taking hold of Damian. *"You must think I'm really stupid!"* he blurted out at Nok.

"No!" Nok's self-satisfied expression of disdain suddenly changed to that of vexation. "I like you! I want you! That why I take you to quiet place in Country Road! But jizz is good! Everyone here take it!"

This comment somehow lightened the pain, but a worrying thought occurred to Damian. He grabbed Nok by the shoulders and pushed her against the back of the sofa. "Did you give me jizz now?"

She was laughing again. "No! I not need to! Jizz is everywhere!"

Damian released her. He was confused. "What do you mean?"

Nok waved her hands in the air at the white mist floating above them. Then Damian realized. *The drug was in the fucking dry ice!*

Stunned, Damian did not resist as it was Nok's turn to push him down onto the sofa. "I know you want me!" she taunted him, as she succeeded in wresting his shorts and underwear from his waist. "Oh my god! You so big!"

"Yes. Thanks to your jizz!" Damian grunted, but did not resist as this new rapacious Nok straddled his legs and grabbed hold of her object of desire.

Damian groaned. He tried to think of Mali … Ursula … but his mind and body were becoming totally transfixed by this sexy Thai vixen, her eyes wide in prurient concentration, tongue licking her upper lip as she massaged him.

Knowing she had complete control over him, Nok stopped what she was doing and raised her hands to her bikini top. "I think you want to see!" she purred.

Damian was, indeed, too entranced to say or do anything. Nok unlatched the bikini releasing those beautiful, perfectly formed breasts. *At last!* was all Damian could think at this point. She began to touch herself, running slim fingers sensuously around her voluptuous curves. Then, she leant down towards Damian, pushing his T-shirt up so that the tips of her provocative bosom brushed against his exposed chest. He was vaguely aware of some of the other naked girls gathering around curiously and beginning to play with themselves as they enjoyed the spectacle. He thought he recognized Mai amongst them, baring an animal-like grin beneath the smears of make-up.

Things were, again, happening far too fast and Damian knew he had to somehow get a hold of himself. He remembered the glinting golden Buddha about Ursula's neck, and focused on the image. With a cry of unrestrained anguish and determination he managed to push himself free of Nok and rolled heavily onto the tiled floor. He staggered awkwardly to his feet, trying to pull his shorts back up, while looking around frantically for a way out of this hell hole, but the glaring lights, grinding music and giggling, voyeuristic Thai females all seemed to be merging into one, completely disorientating him. Damian stumbled forwards, trying to maintain his balance, and then something hit him hard. He realized it was a pillar and he saw a painting of a green snake or serpent wrapped about it with an Asian woman's face, red eyes glaring at him contemptuously, before he painfully collapsed to the floor ...

18 - Perdition

Drifting ... drifting ... towards the billowing clouds of white mist. Raising his arms in submissive acceptance, he allowed the ethereal vapour to wash over him ... engulf him ... cleanse him ... Within, the smiling angels were there to greet him ... reaching out ... caressing his naked body with tender lips and hands. Closing his eyes, he yielded to the sensual delight ... the ecstasy ...

But ... no sooner had it begun ... pleasure turned to pain ... as ... something ... cut into his flesh ... His eyes flashed open to see the angels had become ... demons ... knotted hair flailing ... almond eyes glaring ... and ... sharp, taloned fingers were clawing at him ... long, pointed teeth biting him ... the enticing, voluptuous female bodies now changing ... distorting ... into ... the grotesque ...

A Bangkok Fairy Tale

A distant voice was calling to him ... becoming closer ... then ... blaring music ... blinding lights ...

Damian was back in the Crazy House ...

"Damian! Damian Shoo!"

He looked up to see Nok's concerned face. The past events rushed fuzzily back to the fore of his mind. *Shit!* He lurched upwards in confusion. *How long had he been out for?* His mind was blurred ... unfocused ... He could not remember anything past being on the sofa with Nok ... *It was the drug ...!* He knew he was here for a reason ... *But what was it?!* He dazedly looked around. The dancers were back on the stage – there was nothing more for them to see. Damian looked at his watch ... 9.55 p.m. Thankfully, not too much time had passed ... *or had it ...? Why was he worried about time?* He desperately tried to concentrate his thoughts ... Mali's saddened face flashed into his mind ... *Yes ...! Mali ... Ursula ... Anurak ... They would be waiting for him ... and ... he was supposed to be taking photos ...! He must do it now ... then get the hell out of this place ... and away from the airborne drug ... while he was still alive to tell the tale!*

"Are you OK? Why you run away?" Nok was saying.

Damian groggily raised a finger to his lips to silence her, as he checked his clothes. Fortunately, his shorts and underwear were now safely back in place. Nok must have come to his aid and protected his dignity ... *What was left of it! God! It was Country Road all over again! But ... not really – everyone else was naked this time!*

"Damian!" Nok snapped, impatiently.

"I'm fine," he informed her. "How long was I out for?"

"Not long." She held out an arm to help him up.

Nok's bikini top was back on, but she still looked … *absolutely fantastic …! Dammit!* He had to try and repress these drug-induced provocative feelings … *just a bit longer!* His phone and wallet were still safe in the deep pockets of his khaki shorts. *Good!* No one seemed to be looking at him … except Nok – her expression muddled, confused. *What was he going to do about her?! First things first!* He switched the phone on, wincing at its welcoming chime. Raising it carefully to the dance stage he took a couple of snaps. He was not sure how they would look, but, at least, he had something!

"What you do?" Nok said, screwing her face up, as if trying to focus on him.

"Souvenir," Damian replied, forcing a smile.

Nok looked at him quizzically, and then pinched his backside with a giggle. "Come on. I want to play!"

Damian did not have time for this. "Not now! We have to go! Come on!" he hissed urgently, hiding the phone back in his pocket.

"Why?"

"Trust me!" He grabbed the girl by her arm and guided her into the main area of the bar. It had filled up, which was good – they would not be noticed so much! The customers were both western and Asian, and he could not help but notice the dull, zombie-like look in their eyes. Damian and Nok were now at the edge of the room by an elevator.

"More sexy girls up there!" Nok said, pointing upwards.

Damian looked up to the square, glass floor above. As with the Baccara, he could see between the legs of the naked girls above and paused to watch as another wave of dry ice engulfed him. He felt dizzy.

"We go see!" Nok persevered.

Before Damian could react, Nok had pushed him inside the elevator. He fell back against a silver wall. She fell forward onto him and pressed an illuminated button.

"You like sure!" She squeezed his crutch with a smile.

"Will you stop doing that!"

"You not like me anymore?" Nok replied with a hurt tone.

Damian was groggy. "No …! Yes …! But … we have to get out … of this place!"

With an effort, he slammed his hand onto the elevator's control panel. There was a loud crack and sparks flew followed by the grinding sound of gears awkwardly changing, and then Damian felt a sick sensation of falling. Moments later there was a jarring crash followed by darkness …

The elevator door shakily opened and Damian slumped out. He was hurting all over and his vision was blurred, but he seemed to be in a long, grey, dimly lit corridor. Bare light bulbs stretched out along the low ceiling. A couple of the closer ones were twitching and sparking spasmodically.

He reached out for Nok. She looked unconscious … maybe worse. No. She was still breathing, but there was a nasty looking gash on her forehead. He dragged her out of the elevator and into a sitting position. He slapped her cheek. No response.

Within the dark interior of the elevator Damian could tell its control panel was burnt out. He would have to look for another way out … if he could … and come back for Nok later.

He had an urge to try and contact Mali and tell her what had happened. He checked his phone. *What a surprise! No damn network connection!* He pushed himself painfully to his feet and staggered forward along the corridor. There were a few rusty metal grey doors on the sides of the passageway, but all locked. *Where the hell was he?!*

Finally, he came to a door that was partly opened. He started to push it open further, but stopped when he heard voices ... *speaking English!* He froze. One had a harsh Australian accent. *Could it be the same guy from Country Road?!* He listened further. He could just about make out some words.

"... The next batch needs to be ready tonight!" a German-sounding voice was saying in an urgent tone.

"No worries, mate! I'm onto it!" the Australian replied. "Your stock is ready. Just remember to keep your part of the deal!"

Were they talking about the jizz ... or something else?

The voices became faint and then disappeared. Damian waited a few minutes to be safe, and then eased himself through the door. He seemed to be in some kind of laboratory. *Weird!* The large chamber was filled with what looked like an array of fish tanks bathed in a dim green light, which seemed to be the only form of illumination, and there was a strong smell of formalin. A strange environment to store drugs, Damian thought. No one was to be seen as far as he could tell, and so he cautiously ventured inside. He hobbled over to the nearest tank and peered in. Even in his present numbed state of mind, what he saw greeted him with a nauseating mixture of shock and intense revulsion. He had experienced many things in the short time he had been in this confusing country, but nothing could compare to this ...

At first he thought it was, indeed, a large fish floating in the murky green light, but, as he looked closer, he saw that it definitely was a naked woman. Her flesh was light brown, filmy; the greenness adding an ethereal glow. Eyes were closed and long, dark hair was flailing above her head. She looked beautiful and serene – like a Thai mermaid – but, as he looked further down at the large, voluptuous breasts, he noticed there were ... three of them...

The long, slender legs were crossed at the ankles, and as Damian ran his eyes along them to the waist, he made out a perfect, hairless vagina. But ... there was something else next to it. He squinted into the murkiness and made out ... another perfect, hairless vagina ...

Damian backed away, eyes wide, unbelieving. *Was the jizz he had been subjected to making him hallucinate?!* He looked into another of the fish tanks. The Thai woman looked more or less normal in this one, but then he saw that beneath the hairless vagina was ... a large penis...

He felt he was going to retch and almost knocked over a bell jar. He steadied the jar and saw that it contained another fish-like form, but on closer inspection it seemed to be a human embryo ... with two heads ...

Trying to fight back the panic, Damian moved away into the middle of the room. It was as if he was a part of some living nightmare as he spun around looking into similar fish tanks, each containing its own grotesquery of nature. *Somehow ... he had to keep himself together and take photos of all this sick shit!* But, the overbearing presence of formalin was stinging his eyes and making it even harder not to throw up. He thought of Mali and fumbled for his phone, becoming like some sort of expressionless automaton as he fought back the emotional trauma and began to take snaps of what he could. He came across a stretcher with what looked like a body covered in a grey blanket. Damian faltered as his trembling hand hovered over it, and then, with a grimace, he pulled the blanket back. The bald head of another Thai woman was staring back at him with dead white eyes, and then her black lips pealed open with a snarl, revealing pointed yellow/white teeth.

This was all too much for Damian and he stepped back, dropping his phone and crying out in complete dismay and horror.

"Not fucking you again!" the deep Australian voice said from behind.

A crack of intense pain shot downwards from Damian's head. The last thing he saw was a big man with … an obscenely flattened face … holding … a cricket bat …

Author Biography

Alexander Menyharth is an English/Hungarian writer who has lived and travelled around Thailand, teaching English and writing about his exotic experiences. He has two degrees in psychology and is fascinated by the cultural psyche of the Thai people. Alexander may often be seen in the Bangkok bars and cafés, absorbing the local ambience and gathering inspiration for future writing projects …

I hope you enjoyed reading my book, and, if you have the time, please take a moment to leave a review at ...

Amazon.com/alexander-menyharth/e/B09W32LBGV

Thanks

Alexander Menyharth

Twitter: @AlexMenyharth

Website: alexbrigers.wixsite.com/master-editing

Further titles in the *Land of Poisoned Smiles* trilogy

coming soon ...

Printed in Great Britain
by Amazon